The Quest of the Golden Garter

Novels by Ethel Carnie Holdsworth

Miss Nobody (1913)
Helen of Four Gates (1917)
The Taming of Nan (1919)
The Marriage of Elizabeth (1920)
The House that Jill Built (1920)
Down Poverty Street (1921)
The Great Experiment (1923)
General Belinda (1924)
Equality Island (1925)
This Slavery (1925)
The Quest of the Golden Garter (1927)
Barbara Dennison (1928)
Eagles' Crag (1932)

The Quest of the Golden Garter

Ethel Carnie Holdsworth

with an Introduction
by Amber Stevenson

Kennedy & Boyd,
an imprint of
Zeticula Ltd,
Unit 13,
44-46 Morningside Road,
Edinburgh,
EH10 4BF
Scotland.

http://www.kennedyandboyd.co.uk
admin@kennedyandboyd.co.uk

Frst published in 1927 by Herbert Jenkins
This edition published 2025
Copyright © Estate of Ethel Carnie Holdsworth 2025
Cover photograph © Helen Brown 2025

Paperback ISBN 978-1-84921-253-3

Dedication

To those who dream and live, and work
Amidst hypocrisies and strife,
To build a world for honest folk—
Each giving—jewels of a life,
Yea, pearls of tears for what is lost;
Rubies of heart-blood's bitter flow
For Love, and Life, and Beauty spent
Like hounded crooks, in the world we know.
Still holding fast the spirit's dream—
Howe'er their hands bleed on the way
Dragging firm stone upon firm stone—
The Temple of an unborn Day
O, honest comrades, brave and true,
Who groan, yet build—this book to you.

ETHEL HOLDSWORTH.

Introduction

Amber Stevenson

If Death be equal, why not also life?
Why should the toil, the suffering and the strife
Fall but to some?

wrote Ethel Carnie aged twenty-one in her first poetry collection *Rhymes from the Factory*, articulating from a young age and the outset of her career a strong sense of social justice that persisted throughout her life. Born in 1886 in Lancashire, the daughter of millworkers, Carnie herself began work in a mill aged just eleven. Despite receiving little formal education, she developed a love of writing and continued her learning, going on to be one of the first working-class female novelists and an activist, poet, and editor in an extraordinary trajectory. Writing and publishing poetry while working in the mill, she caught the attention of socialist Robert Blatchford, who hired her at *The Woman Worker*, following which she was able to leave the factory and relocate to London. Their relationship soon fell apart, however, as her outspoken views on women's rights and fierce critique of capitalism clashed with Blatchford's image of her as 'a Lancashire fairy' as he described her, and she was fired within six months of starting the position. She went on to found her own anti-fascist paper, *The Clear Light*, which ran between 1923 and 1925, and over the course of her career published thirteen novels, several poetry collections, and was involved with the Independent Labour Party, the Co-operative movement, and passionately campaigned for gender and social equality, pacificism, and Marxism.

Despite her radical work and unprecedented achievements, her literary and political contributions have largely been forgotten. Aside from some poetry and the republication of her more commercially and critically successful novels *Helen of Four Gates* (1917) and *This Slavery* (1925), until recently her works have been almost inaccessible to modern readers and in the mid 2000s no copyright library held all of her works. Why has Ethel Carnie Holdsworth's legacy disappeared from working-class literary history and histories of the socialist, anti-war, and women's movements of the early twentieth century? Perhaps forgotten is the wrong word to use. Histories of slavery and marginalised groups have demonstrated the archive is not a politically neutral space but is capable of enacting epistemic violence on its subjects. Through the selection and exclusion of materials certain narratives become privileged which often support institutional or official ones.

Scholars have speculated on why Carnie Holdsworth and her writing are largely absent from historical memory. Her fiction routinely experimented with form and genre, incorporating social realism, crime, and melodrama, united by the common threads of romance and an exploration of class and gender inequalities. She understood the radical potential of fiction and poetry as means of raising political consciousness and wove her views into all of her creative work. Her playful use of genre may have contributed to her present obscurity, as her work refused to fit neatly into genre categories. Carnie Holdsworth was also not intimately involved with major socialist and feminist organisations of the period; thus, her legacy was not preserved through institutional archives.

I would also add that Carnie Holdsworth has in part been marginalised by history because she did not lead a traditional middle-class life even as she entered what was and still is a middle-class profession. Similarly, Ann Quin, writing in the mid twentieth century, offered a radically different working-class voice that was avant-garde, surreal, and disruptive. There has been some recent examination of her legacy, but Quin has been left out of the experimental canon. Both were women who experienced poverty and economic precarity while celebrated as authors, and Holdsworth remained outside the literary establishment. The amnesia in literary history of working-class fiction authors has had a profound impact beyond obscuring their literary contributions. Class prejudice persists both in history and literary studies on the ability of the working class to write articulately and imaginatively and have subsequently neglected the application of literary methodologies to their work, using working-class life writing in particular for its content and ignoring form. Carnie Holdsworth and Quin's erasure from literary histories in some ways validates these claims, and greater attention to their talents may hopefully encourage a re-evaluation of writing by members of the working class more broadly.

Unlike many of her earlier novels which were situated within working-class communities, *The Quest of the Golden Garter* moves away from the family, factory life, industrial labour, and union organising to the glamour and excess of the London upper classes. In one of her more stylised works, we are introduced to Billy Durant, handsome and charming but chronically lazy and growing tired of his life of privilege which provides him little excitement. At the opening of the novel, he begins to yearn for something more than 'eating forever and jading [himself] with shows', when during a stroll in the park he stumbles upon a yellow silk garter with the name and address of Lydia Carstairs embroidered upon its lining. Viewing this as an opportunity for adventure, he sets out to find its owner, and upon meeting her is quickly besotted and becomes entangled in a criminal scheme robbing his friends and family of their jewels.

Golden Garter was published during the 'golden age' of crime and detective fiction, Agatha Christie having published her first novel in 1920 and Dorothy L. Sayers in 1923. It is understandable that Carnie Holdsworth, known for her experimentation with genre, would try her hand at crime fiction as a means of broadening her audience. What struck me about The Quest of the Golden Garter is the ferocity with which she criticises the greed and ignorance of the wealthy to the plight of the poor. Her attempt at reaching a wider and more diverse readership does not soften her social critique. Golden Garter is ultimately a story in which a young woman is corrupted by the city, as Lydia comes to London in the hopes of becoming a singer but, after being pickpocketed and attempting to pickpocket herself, is entrapped by her intended victim, Shaney/Jenkins in the 'Golden Garter Gang'. She directs her anger and frustration about her predicament towards Billy as he professes his love for her. 'What have you and such as you to do with such as us?... You ride on the spray of life, all flashing and rainbow-hued! You float on top of us, drowning below in the gulfs, and you do not know we are there, until we rise like vultures and pick off the gold you are gilded with or the jewels you wear.' (p.46) It is clear Carnie Holdsworth was always writing firstly for her own people, articulating particular structures of feeling including anger and a profound sense of difference that were key in working class resistance of the period.

Within the confines of the setting, it is difficult for Carnie Holdsworth to fully articulate her political vision, however. Despite the caustic indictments delivered by Lydia, they lose some of their potency and specificity as the novel does not do much, or even attempt, to convince the reader of the ways in which the wealthy are complicit in the oppression and dispossession of the working classes. *This Slavery* involves a violent confrontation between factory workers and owner and the reader is shown on a personal level the violence and oppression embedded into relations between workers and their employers. In *The Quest of the Golden Garter,* however, we seem to be expected to accept the premise the wealthy are inherently evil, even while Carnie Holdsworth writes upper class characters who are for the most part benign and at their worst showy and selfish.

Similarly, while Billy's encounter with Lydia transforms his world view, he does not really do anything with his newly discovered empathy. Billy initially pushes away thoughts of the suffering of others, thinking to himself in the opening pages 'that grim and sordid struggles...must be going on. Then, because thinking tired him, he shrugged his shoulders. What was it to do with him, after all?' (p.4) Later, however, following Lydia's meeting in which she scolds his 'lot' for their indifference, he remembers the deaths of nine miners trapped in a burning mine and 'his life felt suddenly flimsy, worthless, weighed against the heroism of the nine trapped men. Felt ignoble, rotten, vicious, not worth mentioning.' (p.41) His only real 'noble' act, following this revelation, however, is to go along with the Golden Garter gang's ploy once he discovers it rather than reporting the Lydia and her conspirators to the police and to those around him. These actions appear more motivated by his love for her, rather than a newly found sense of social justice. And love does not overcome class in *Golden Garter*. Rather, Lydia's inheritance facilitates her social ascent. It is therefore a novel of individual social advancement and assimilation into the upper classes that is depicted as wholly uncomplicated, and one in which class is constructed as a purely economic relation.

The book is also overstuffed with plot: at less than a hundred and seventy pages in this edition, so much happens that as a reader, I found myself at times a bit lost in some of the twists and fast changing focalisations between characters. *Golden Garter* is not entirely centred around the gang and their criminal activity: in the action of the final third we leave London behind and follow Lydia to the coast. After the group is dispersed following the shooting of a detective at their last robbery, Shaney flees with Lydia out of the city. Hiding out in an abandoned house during a storm, Shaney suffers a stroke, and in her search for help during the night Lydia loses her grip of reality, entering a kind of fugue state. She is taken in by a fishing community where she remains for three months, mute, until upon hearing the name Billy her faculties are restored. She learns she is near to the village in which she grew up, and upon returning learns of the deaths of her caretakers, her two aunts, who have left her a sizeable inheritance. Her face, however, is heavily scarred from exposure to the harsh winds and sea during her catatonia, and flees from Billy, and with her new wealth receives singing training and establishes herself as a successful masked opera singer known as Madame Mascari. Billy, who had previously heard her sing, attends one of her concerts and immediately recognises her voice. At the resolution of the novel, they are finally reunited and Mascari's true identity kept secret from those she previously stole from. All of this takes place within the last fifty pages and feels incredibly rushed and jars with the rest of the text.

Excepting the more solemn final third, *The Quest of the Golden Garter* is a lively romp that has an escapist charm in its decadence and at times absurd plotting. The London we see is not the grey, smog filled streets of squalor in much Victorian and Edwardian fiction, but is verdant, extravagant, almost magical, the Savoy being transformed into Venice in one scene, in which the guests drift upon gondolas among islets and 'great sprays of mimosa'. For many of her contemporary readers from the working class, the world in which *Golden Garter* largely takes place was so alien to them that in this almost mythic register members of the lower classes could change the paths life had laid out for them.

Carnie Holdsworth was also doing what no other authors were doing at the time: writing stories *about* working-class women, *for* working-class women. She articulated their individual subjectivities and desires outside the confines of the dominant class culture. Carnie Holdsworth's creativity and talent saved her from a life in the factory or domestic service, the former which she described as having 'crushed the childhood, youth, maturity of millions of men and women,' understanding both as forms of slavery. For nearly all poor women of this period, however, this was an impossibility, and their lives were predetermined by the social and economic position into which they were born. Contemporary class culture situated them in a collectivity within which there was little space for their own desires. Marriage was seen to serve a pragmatic function for them in the early twentieth century, providing greater economic security rather than a relation based upon romantic love and emotional fulfilment. Carnie Holdsworth in her fiction creates a space in which their romantic and individual fantasies are not only expressed but actualised.

Unlike many of her male contemporaries and institutions on the left, Carnie Holdsworth did not let class supersede issues of gender. She understood that work was not the only place in which women could be enslaved but also in intimate relations with men. Violence in the late nineteenth and early twentieth centuries was normalised to the extent that it was widely viewed as a central part of masculine identity, and until the mid-twentieth century was seen as characteristic of the working-class. The language of coercive control in romantic relationships did not however exist until the late twentieth century and silence surrounded public discourse on domestic violence, which largely went unpoliced. Carnie Holdsworth broke that silence, rendering vividly the psychic toll physical and emotional abuse can take on its victims. Shaney physically assaults Lydia and manipulates her into marrying him and becoming involved in his criminal scheme. In one scene Lydia begs Shaney to kill her, her life having been reduced to such misery by his entrapment, and her faith having been 'almost destroyed' by him. She is not a passive victim of Shaney, though, insisting she would commit suicide before spending the rest of her life married to him.

While Shaney reflects dominant ideas about working-class masculinity in his violent outbursts towards Lydia, Slimmy, another member of the Golden Garter Gang, embodies a softer form of masculinity. He is perceptive, sensitive, and deeply protective of Lydia, presenting an alternative way of being a man that distances itself from aggression and brutality. In her portrayal of the ways in which men oppress women and constructs different forms of masculinity emerge some of Carnie Holdsworth's most radical social commentary and critique in *Golden Garter*.

The incredible and unprecedented achievements of Ethel Carnie Holdsworth are well overdue proper recognition and celebration. The republication of her novels feels timely in an economic climate in which it is becoming increasingly challenging to sustain a career in the arts. A recent *The Guardian* article reported that less than one in ten workers in the arts come from working class backgrounds, and huge cuts across the sector are making it increasingly inaccessible and unsustainable for those without access to other sources of wealth and established connections to the industry. While her political messaging gets somewhat muddled in the narrative in *The Quest of the Golden Garter* and is perhaps one of her less politically radical or affecting novels, Carnie Holdsworth imagines working-class women like Lydia, and herself, who refuse to be bound to societal expectations and strive for more than life has given them. It is a joy to read the work of an author who represented unseen lives, desires, and experiences. Her words resonate just as powerfully today in an era of widening wealth inequality:

More! Though the people faint beneath a load
Of unrequired labour, further goad;
Drive us more quickly up life's hill
Ye rich! that ye may reap more profit still.

Relentlessly, as vinters crush the grape
Beneath their heel they press us out shape:
Their brothers, children of one parent Vine,
And care not, whilst they quaff Life's richest wine.

TO-DAY AND TO-MORROW

Where those who rob the poor and weak,
Until that hour when they are strong,
Walk with a proud and blushless cheek,
"Law" on their side, and Force of Wrong;
Where "thief" robs "thief" of high degree
Of jewels that robbed men of life,
And not one soul knows Liberty
Midst blood and sand of Greed and Strife,
I lift a banner white as morn
Which says that all men are opprest,
Tyrant or slave, so soon as born—
Like infants for their mother's breast
Fighting their way with desperate hands
Still unappeased, perverted, sad,
Till slaves shall burst their spirit's bands,
Freemen, who shout with laughter glad,
"Here is our Mother, yea, the Earth,
Where honest men bring better Birth."

THE QUEST OF THE GOLDEN GARTER

CHAPTER I

He stared into the blue dusk of the London evening, wondering how he should pass the hours before the morning which would bring Carminetta's answer. On that answer, Billy was quite sure hung the thread of his destiny. As yet he was drifting idly with the tides.

Immaculately attired, cultured to the last zenith, young, living easily on money as to the sources of which he was too refined to inquire, Billy Durant had made a pleasant stir when his Aunt steered him into the maelstrom of their social set, with the quaint introduction, "Here's Billy, who fails at everything, but is such a clever boy, really." It was perhaps his air of extreme pleasure in laziness which had captured the bored set. Then he had met Carminetta, one of the year's debutantes, and had fallen a victim to life's first unrest. He was awaiting her answer to a vital question, popped as he had almost lifted her into her furred cloak—a question to which she had only answered, "I'll write you in a week, Billy dear" though he felt quite sure she might have answered then and there had that antique cat, Lady Dandover, not swooped down to take charge of Carminetta: very like a spectacled hawk in satin and pearls sweeping down on an irised wood-pigeon, Billy had thought.

He went all over it again, staring into the blue dusk, where the lights of London were caught in the net of the trees in the Gardens before the Crescent. He wondered, irrelevantly, hand tapping the polished table by which he sat, if *all* London was dining! Even the Billy Durants sometimes wonder about vital things, though quite irrelevantly. Away beyond that belt of lights, like a Milky Way come to earth, he realised that grim and sordid struggles to exist must be going on. Then, because thinking tired him, he shrugged his shoulders. What was it to do with him, after all?

"Nothing, Billy," he answered himself, lightly. "Nothing at all."

With his careless grace, the birthright of a long line of careless "disgraces," he went down and found his hat in the hall. At least, Ambrose, the wooden-faced footman, found it and volunteered the information that "It is raining just a little, sir," handing him his mackintosh.

Aunt Kate, thought Billy caustically, must have powers of clairvoyance. She swooped out of the dining-room and caught him as he was opening the door.

"Not going out, Billy, surely?" she enquired.

"Must have a breather, Aunt."

The radiance from the arc light before the door fell on his young face. Aunt Kate realised that he was the most handsome creature the Durant family had produced and they were a handsome lot. She had really counted on Billy meeting her new acquaintances, the Willards. After all, millionaires did not grow on trees, nor millionaires' daughters.

"All your favourite dishes to-night, too, Billy, dear," she reproached him, in her exquisite voice.

Billy lifted an eyebrow.

"Aunt, I shall finish up with gastritis," he pleaded.. "No, I must go out. These indoor hours are making me feel stupid."

She button-holed him, playfully.

"You'll drop in before the last course, Billy?" she begged. "There are some delightful people I want you to meet."

Billy surveyed her.

"If you could find me some truly undelightful people, I could be more enthusiastic," was his comment. "Delightful people *get* stale after a time."

She laughed. Billy had to be humoured to be captured.

"These are distinctly original," she told him. "Do drop in."

Billy promised, in order to escape.

His aunt knew that it was only to escape, but Billy had one virtue not common to either the stock he came of, or their social set. He kept the tiniest suggestion of a promise.

With a sense of relief young Durant closed the carved door behind him and passed out into the road, and as the gate of the Crescent Gardens was not passed in. There were swans on the silver disc of the pond, over which the pale, shimmering willows leaned. Sunset was beginning to burn. The laburnum shook its "golden rain" over his head. He drew a profound sigh of relief once again, watching the reflection of the swans in the water. Proud-necked birds they were, thought Billy, the aristocrats of London. But he liked the sparrows better, always on the scramble to live, yet cocky and cheerful as you please. One or two hopped close to his feet. He took out the bag he always brought with him for the Garden sparrows. The swans he considered were well-fed enough.

"Excuse me, could you tell me where Crescent Mansions are? I'm quite lost, I think," said a voice almost in his ear, as he was occupied with the crumbs.

He looked up.

Through the gloaming he saw an exquisitely attired young lady regarding him with interest. She wore a hat which shadowed her face, but he could not miss the wonder of her large eyes, softly brilliant, and the dusky cloud of her hair, unbobbed, caught at his lazy appreciation.

"There are Crescent Mansions," he told her, rising to his feet, and pointing lazily.

"It is Number Seven," she told him. "In the dusk one cannot see the numbers."

"Aunt Kate is at Number Seven. An arc light, and the monkey-puzzle in the garden, will lead you to it," he said nonchalantly.

"Then you are——"

She paused.

"I'm Billy Durant, at the present moment rather tired of him," Billy told her, smiling, and quite unaware of how handsome he was when smiling.

She considered him for a moment.

Such a confidence called for another.

"I'm Lilian Harding," she told him. "And I'm never tired of being Lilian Harding. Thanks so much. No, don't come with me. I see you prefer—sparrows!"

There was a mixture of frankness and subtlety in her parting shot. He watched her disappear, not without some interest, not quite forgetting her, but realising that she would be pretty much like all the other young ladies he had seen, once she got into the setting of his Aunt Kate's stale gatherings. He left the Gardens and walked to the nearest tube.

He sauntered through the tiled hollows, studying the review pictures, and realising that he was losing his enthusiasm for shows, that life was becoming unreal and losing its freshness that, horror of horrors, he was becoming bored.

"A man should do something," he mused. "With Carminetta I believe I could find things in life, besides eating forever and jading myself with shows."

He studied the people rushing past him along the tube-ways. A rustling female in silk dress swept past him, then a commercial traveller, a little worn and anxious looking, carrying a brown bag. Next passed a woman with three little children who looked as though they had been having a day in the country, the children now tired, and crying, the woman appealing, and all understanding of their weariness.

"I'll carry your bundle," declared Billy.

She stopped and stared at him.

"Oh, thanks, we're all right," she said. "We can manage."

Suspicion! He saw it in her tired look. After all, he could not blame her. London *was* a strange place, where it would seem strange that one of a jostling, hurrying throng would offer a hand to carry another's burden even to the train. Yes. There must be *strange* things going on in London, even at this very moment, unbelievable things, adventures more fantastic than any picture in any show. He wished he could find some of it, but so far it had avoided him. Perhaps if he dressed like an Apache it might meet him, he mused disconsolately.

Then he stepped on it.

His-first action was to kick it, schoolboy fashion.

But he saw that it was a "thing of beauty" and that it was quite inappropriate to kick it.

He stooped and picked it up, impeding the progress of a man rushing for the Chalk Farm train, smiled apologies at the most extreme language, and studied the find.

A garter.

A Golden Garter, with capital letters.

Quite definitely *a young lady's Garter.* (He had studied French.) A slim young lady, decided Billy.

And a rather unusual young lady, at that.

It was created of yellow silk with a dewdrop jewel in each rose. Yes. "Created" was the word. It had never been made.

An extravagant, young lady, rather, thought Billy, still day-dreaming, as he held it in slack hand.

Just then a sickly looking elderly clerk brushed past him.

Billy felt irresponsible, as when College rags had engaged him, not long since, yet an age ago, as life is reckoned.

He wanted to see what the elderly clerk's face would look like when surprised out of its apathy. He hurried after him.

"Excuse me! Have you lost anything?" inquired Billy, politely, and now feeling young once more.

The clerk whizzed round.

"Lost anything?" he growled. "I'd have to find something to lose first!"

Then he gasped, regarding the Garter in the hand of Billy, the Garter dangling out ridiculously, almost melodramatically.

"Gammon!" he said angrily. "I haven't time to play with boys. I've a train to catch. Drinking, that's what you've been. Some of you don't know how to get your time over. Mine's all spoken for. You and your d—d garter!"

Billy's laughter followed him as he dashed along the tube-ways.

He tried it on several people, who apparently regarded him as either intoxicated or insane and were all sadly lacking in humour, but when a stout mater-familias told him he ought to be ashamed of himself and threatened to report him for indecency, whilst Billy said the Garter was most decent, the fit of exhilarated irresponsibility had passed. It was then that he examined it in detail and found that inside it, on a band of yellow silk elastic, was a small tab on which was the name and address of the owner. It was then that Billy scented possible adventure. He had, moreover, been introduced to so many young ladies against his will that to seek one out and introduce himself to her against her will had an element of attraction.

Lydia Carstairs sounded both practical and romantic. Lydia suggested poetry, Carstairs suggested blue-bookishness, and an ancient lineage, with yew tree and elegant swans in parks.

Billy found himself travelling towards her before he realised it. The Golden Garter dropped on the arid stones of a tiled tube-way had already commenced its spell. He was acute enough to know that it might be a designed spell. Young ladies of respectable origin take care not to drop Golden Garters which connote their names and addresses unless there is something weird and wonderful behind such actions.

Anyhow, it would pass the hours, the eternal hours between now and when Carminetta would perhaps say "yes" and save him from personal adventures in quest of romance hung on so dainty and daring an object as a garter.

"Yes. This is the flat of Miss Lydia Carstairs," Billy was told, as he stood on the very real doorstep which he saw had been recently cleaned.

"I have—er—found something of value to her—at least—" said Billy, faltering a little, quite unusually.

The footman was quite unlike any footman Billy had seen. He looked as though he had been one of Gilbert and Sullivan's Yeomen of the Guards, a great fellow, who would most certainly have had to be measured for his livery of crimson and white. On his sleeve (Billy could scarcely credit his eyes) was a yellow rose (embroidered), evidently the coat of arms of the establishment. He suddenly appreciated the sense of humour of a young lady who embroidered footmen to match her garters. The footman, he felt, was examining him as keenly as he was examining the footman. There were yellow roses in a black jar on a small black table, and the tall lamp had yellow roses on its coppery coloured glasses.

"I will give it to Miss Carstairs," said the footman.

"I prefer to hand it to Miss Carstairs herself," Billy told him sternly. The footman did a most unfootmanlike thing; he shrugged his great shoulders.

"I will bring Miss Carstairs. Pass into that room," he said with another glance at Billy, much as a super-man might glance at something of no importance, thought Billy, angrily. He passed into the room, and sat himself down. It was all in black and yellow, to the smallest detail. A room in those colours gave one a curious sensation of the environment of a black and yellow snake, and Billy began to realise that this was certainly no orthodox house. Why, the very cat had something weird about it, long, yellow and black itself, sinuous, almost sinister.

Then he heard footsteps and forgot the cat and the room.

She came into the place, nodded at him casually, turned up the light of the electric lamp on the table, and said a trifle wearily: "John tells me you have found something of mine. I am not aware that I have lost anything of *any value.*"

Billy's mind was whirling in all directions.

Whirling more than when he had met Carminetta.

Yet all he was conscious of was a young woman in a black velvet dress, which fitted her like a sheath, whilst above it arose a proudly poised head, with black curly hair of the black that is like a cloud rather than burnished, and a pair of dark eyes, a little tired, set in the pallor of a face whose clear paleness showed up the exquisite colour of the most maddening mouth Billy had ever seen. White poppies! That was what she made him think of. White poppies by a moonlit sea. White poppies with shadowy, beautiful hearts. Magic poppies, for the dreaming of men. He actually found himself stammering un-Billyishly. He felt hot to have to refer to a—a—Garter. He realised that the stout woman in the tube-way had been right. Only a male ape could have jested on so sacred a thing as *her* Garter.

"Yes, I am Miss Carstairs," she told him.

"I—er—found an article," began Billy. "At least—I think I found it—or—I mean, of course—"

She surveyed him with maddening casualness. Must take him for a complete ass!

She even yawned.

"Let us *hope* you found it after it was lost," she said smiling, and he realised that when she smiled, she could drive men, some men, of course—frantic.

"Oh, it was *after* it was lost," said Billy. "It's rather—an—er—unmentionable sort of article."

He was glad now he had wrapped it up in his handkerchief to make it more presentable.

He held it out, and discovered that his hand was not quite steady.

"I am not aware " she began.

Then she unfolded the handkerchief.

"Oh!" she ejaculated and stared down at it without a flicker of an eyelid. "Yes. This is mine. How careless of me! Thanks so much. I am sorry—"

"I'd consider it no trouble to bring it a thousand miles!" burst out Billy, enthusiastically.

She paused at that, smiled at the ridiculousness of him, and seemed to consider him more closely.

"I really would," said Billy impetuously.

She opened a cigarette case and offered him a cigarette. Once she flashed a look at the door, as though afraid someone might be listening.

"You have one of these," said Billy. "They're heavenly."

She took one. He lit it for her.

It all seemed suddenly the most natural thing in the world that he should be sitting on a yellow and black couch, lighting a cigarette for her. That was the strangest thing about it.

"Wait a moment," she said, and went swiftly out of the room. Billy felt that she was looking to see if the footman was gone. She came in with a calmer face.

Then, without altering her restful position, without any sign that it was not the most usual thing in the world to say, she observed:

"Don't be tempted to call again. Things are not what they seem here. I didn't mean *you* to find that *thing*. Be warned."

They heard the door-bell ring.

"There *he* is," she said.

Her tone was indescribable. .

"Leave now," she urged Billy.

There was the first frantic note in her tone he had heard.

"There's a side door," she informed him quietly. "Get out, now."

But Billy did not move.

Someone was coming, whistling in very commonplace fashion.

"Ah! There you are, Lydia, my dear," said a man's voice. "I have ordered you —"

Then he stopped with real or simulated surprise. Billy was almost sure it was simulated, but not quite sure. He was getting badly mixed.

"Father, this young man found something I had lost," said Lydia, rising from the couch. "He has only just arrived."

Her father bowed.

He was a most classical-looking individual.

He murmured a few words about the weather.

"I'll leave you now," said Billy politely.

The classic-looking man was regarding him.

"Oh, don't run away like that," he said with gracious politeness. "We get so few young men here, that we must be gracious to them. Lydia, ring for food."

"But the young man has a vital appointment," said Lydia, blushlessly. "He has promised to call again in a few days."

Billy nodded, with all the feelings of an intelligent shuttlecock being battledored from one to the other.

"Oh, we must not interfere with vital appointments," said the father. "Lydia, John has gone out. You may show our visitor to the door."

Billy found himself following her.

She turned, and at the door laid her fingers across her lips to signal him to silence.

Her tremulous whisper came to him.

"Don't come again—"

His eyes reassured her, and her smile, grateful, wonderful, essence of a strange lotus-like sweetness, meshed him round.

The door closed behind him.

Then he found that Carminetta's voice was sounding on his ears, startlingly banal.

"Why, Billy dear," she was saying. "What are you doing here?"

"I—er—was just strolling round," he told her.

"How lucky," she said. "And Billy dear, I need not write now—" She was looking fondly at him, in quite moving earnestness, yet trying to smile.

To his horror, his intense horror he realised that he was dreadfully afraid she was going to say "Yes" to that vital question, which he had put—why, sometime during "yesterday's seven thousand years."

CHAPTER II

With a feeling of inexplicable relief Billy listened to Carminetta's explanation. They walked on as she gave it. She had promised Lady Dandover to be quite free for a year, at least, as they were both quite young and had scarcely seen anyone else.

"Yes, I think that will be best," Billy agreed, joyfully, his heart pounding relief. Trim in her tailor-made costume, and the hat which gave no sign of having cost fifteen guineas, Billy saw that Carminetta certainly was much like her father, one of the big city bankers. Her practicality, her banality, suddenly jarred on him. They walked to the Embankment, and leaning over the parapet admired the lights reflected in the water. It was only then that Billy recalled he was due back for the last course.

"You come back with me!" commanded Billy. "There's a millionaire to supper. Come and look at it, Car."

He realised that he was indeed still rather fond of Carminetta.

But something had happened to him, since he had met the lady of the Garter. He was more mixed up than in his first struggles with Euclid.

"But I promised Lady Dandover," began Carminetta, hesitantly.

"Oh, hang Lady Dandover. Come on. We can just do it," urged Billy.

Had he not been in a mental and moral mix-up, consequent on having realised that there were moons of beauty which made the stars pale, he might have noticed that it took all Carminetta's control not to break down and cry in a London thoroughfare. She had realised, as she laid her hand on his sleeve and said that she need not write, that Billy had regretted his enthusiastic proposal in the conservatory. After all—, she had discounted something of it before, had realised the effect of the music, the warmth, the gay parade of youth, the sense of drifting on lotus-stream which ran one knew not where.

She wanted to sniff, pitiably, like any jilted shopgirl, or at the very least she wanted very badly to run away, and escape from Billy, who did not realise how relieved he had looked to get a year's reprieve.

"Yes. Do come on," urged Billy.

"Let's run."

He flashed her the old Billyish look of affection.

She ran after him, laughing, to the tube, and they jumped on the train at the peril of being jammed by the gates. Billy took out his paper.

Carminetta's brain was working quickly.

Something had happened to Billy since last she saw him, and the something was a woman, of course. It was going to be a desperate fight to land Billy, and she was summing up any possible odds against her. She was cheerfully and unromantically pretty,—and they were fond of each other in the way that spelt true happiness.

But she might be up against someone rather unscrupulous. Billy was rather stupidly honest. It was one of his attractions. She pondered him for the first time, as a riddle which had to be quickly solved.

"Naughty, naughty," Billy's Aunt told them. "We're half way through the last course, but come along in. Oh, Carminetta, how are you?"

She kissed Carminetta with the tolerant affection which held in reserve the idea that providing Billy could do no better, Carminetta was not so bad, really, and well worth being in the running.

"You look headachy, my dear," she said.

"We've been running," explained Carminetta.

"You shouldn't let Billy run you, it's bad for the heart, and—you look best unflushed," commented Billy's Aunt.

"Now, in you go, both of you."

Billy winked at Carminetta before pushing the door open. He leaned his mouth to her ear and whispered, realising that it was certainly a very pretty pinky sort of ear.

"Don't lose your heart to the millionaire, Car. It might be a pig in a poke," he warned her.

Then he opened the door, the best mannered boy in the world, and Carminetta entered.

Cheney, in the post of honour at the table, saw a pretty girl come to dine in a white blouse and serge skirt, a girl with a flushed face and quiet eyes, who crept into her place like one who wished to avoid notice. Then he saw Billy, and said "So!" under his breath. Billy was certainly dashing enough to make up for Carminetta's almost schoolgirlish shyness, and the atmosphere of nursery and jam-teas which yet clung to her despite her having been "out" half a season. In her flutter of nervousness she had taken her hostess's vacant chair. He was near though now to observe quite critically that she was indeed well worth looking at. Beside her Lilian Harding seemed sophisticated, and a little worn. That young lady was at her second glass of champagne, and repartee was passing across the table between her and Billy, and Carminetta was watching them, fearfully, jealously, under school-girl's furtive eyelashes, and not interested in Cheney at all. Which gave an odd pang to Cheney.

"Just out, aren't you?" queried Cheney, sympathetically.

Carminetta fixed the glance of her quiet grey eyes upon the millionaire. She noted that he was the most ugly man she had ever seen, outside Grimm's ogres.

"H'm, yes," she said, blushing, and a little indignant.

He enjoyed the spark in her eyes.

"And what do you think of it?" he enquired.

"Really, I don't know yet," Carminetta told him guardedly; and suddenly thought Lilian Harding looked rather pathetic.

Presently they filed into the drawing room and Carminetta listened distractedly to the millionaire, whilst Miss Harding sang wild Persian love-songs and Billy turned the pages for her.

"You must come to see my daughter," Cheney Willard told Carminetta. "She's quite ruined and spoiled. Perhaps you'd do her good. And if you could possibly get her to walk I'd be everlastingly grateful, for she's getting too fat, to put it brutally. Nice young man, this Billy boy, isn't he?"

"Very," said Carminetta, casually.

Cheney Willard admired her more and more.

"If I could marry her off to someone she'd dote on, someone without much money," said Cheney thoughtfully, leaning his arm on the back of Carminetta's chair, "it would be her salvation. Is this Billy boy engaged?"

Carminetta regarded him calmly.

"Not that I'm aware of," she said, disinterestedly.

Then they heard the voice of Billy's Aunt.

"Yes. It's quite true. Another mansion robbery, Kensington district this time. Jewels! They never take anything else. And though a vigorous inspection of letters is being made, nothing has been found, though the widespread nature of the robberies points to collaboration from different areas. It's frightful."

Cheney Willard looked in an amused way at Billy's Aunt. Then he turned to Carminetta again.

Fantastic, as the notion seemed, he was really falling in love with Carminetta, a girl barely tolerated by his hostess as in the running for Billy. Falling in love with a girl in a white blouse and serge skirt, who had sat in the wrong chair at dinner? When Cheney got an idea he hung on to it, however odd it was.

"So, bring this Billy boy friend of yours round to our shant, say Wednesday," he urged. "And you'll both meet Poppy. No. She's decidedly nicer than I am or Billy boy wouldn't look at her."

He laughed, seeing that he had answered

Carminetta's thoughts written so plainly, for a moment, on her face. He urged the point until, without actual rudeness, Carminetta could not refuse.

When at last she was free to depart, he found Willard also saying good-bye, and he urged that he could run her along in the car, Miss Harding too, Billy also, and drop them out, one by one. They were all hustled in. Miss Harding simulated shyness, but Carminetta felt the glance of the half-shut eyes upon her, upon Billy, upon Willard, and did not like her.

"So you are to come along and meet my Poppy," said Cheney, slapping Billy on the back. "We'll expect you at three on Wednesday. Miss Dawson and I have fixed it all up."

Carminetta nodded, and felt trapped.

Lilian Harding leaned forward, sleepily.

"And what have I done?" she enquired, "And I'd so like to see the inside of a millionaire's house."

Cheney Willard laughed.

"Do come, too, Miss Harding," he told her, "I didn't mean to be rude."

Then he put out Miss Harding, and there was only Billy and Carminetta, who suddenly decided they would get out together, and walk to Carminetta's house.

Cheney Willard complied.

They watched his car disappear, one of many others, moving stars, along the road.

"Where did Miss Harding drop from?" inquired Billy.

Carminetta shook her head.

"I was going to ask you," she told him.

"Well, she's evidently plenty of pluck," said Billy admiringly. "I wonder if she golfs."

"I really can't inform you," Carminetta told him. "There's something queer about her."

"I found her distinctly original," challenged Billy. "By the way, is it you or I whom Willard really desires to get to this tea-party business?"

"You, I should say," said Carminetta.

"Sure?" enquired Billy.

"Sure!" answered Carminetta, honestly, keeping Willard's words in her mind. She could not tell Billy that Willard had him in mind as a possible son-in-law to be the salvation of a spoiled daughter. And once more the face of Willard, ugly, like a chunk of rock, hammered crudely, rose up before her. She thought she rather liked him.

"Billy, I won't walk. Get me a taxi," she ordered.

She felt sleepy, weary, all at once, and wanted to be quiet, so that she could think. All was jumbled, as in the head of a bewildered, jaded child, a mix-up in which she saw Miss Harding drinking champagne and making eyes at Billy— with an unknown Poppy, defined as "ruined" by her own father, looming up on the; horizon; with Billy getting distracted fits in which it was plain his thoughts were elsewhere. She was only nineteen, and wanted to be home, and go to bed and cry.

Billy put her into the taxi, lifted his hat, and she was whirled away. Once in the corner of the taxi she covered her face with her hands, and wept bitterly. Billy had been her first dream. And something or someone had come across its fulfilment. Already she saw him vanishing from her world.

As for Billy he walked on and on, towards Marble Arch. In the glow of the lights one could sense the full beauty of Spring in Hyde Park, large, and green, and spacious. And a pale face of lotus-like beauty loomed up before him, beckoning him on like a siren, yet saying with human lips of warning, "Don't come again." And even with these thoughts in his mind, he ran into "them," the second of two curious coincidences that night. To look for anyone in London is to seek a needle in a hay stack. Yet, first, he had met Carminetta, as he had left the house of mystery. And now he saw her again. She was standing by a waiting taxi, in company with a young man, very tall and gentlemanly. And her voice was no longer the voice of the gentle charmer who had warned him not to come to the house again.

"I refuse to do it," she was saying vehemently. "Absolutely, do you hear, Jenkins? You can tell the rest *that*. You can threaten as you like, you and all the rest of you. I refuse to do it."

Jenkins laughed.

He merely rearranged the light coat on his arm.

"But Lydia," he appealed.

Don't 'Lydia' me," she told him. "Oh, I'm sick of it all, sick of it, sick to death of it. I wish I had never been born."

She had turned, but Jenkins followed, easily, rapidly and laid a restraining hand on her arm.

"This is the last time," Billy heard him say. "The very last. We are out of it, after this. They've agreed. Lydia, be sensible. Think on. Buckingham Palace Gardens, at four to-morrow afternoon 'without fail!"

She gave Jenkins a despairing glance, shook hands with him, stepped into the taxi and off it went, leaving Billy with a fleeting impression of her sitting back in it like a statue of despair. As for Billy, he watched the departing Jenkins, whoever he really was, with feelings akin to murder. And he resolved, at all hazards, to be at the house he had been warned from, and to keep her there, till after four on the morrow.

****

"Another!" almost shouted. Billy's Aunt, from the head of the breakfast table.

"Another what?" inquired Billy, yawning.

"Jewel robbery," she gasped. 'It's dreadful."

"Flowers will be fashionable in a little while," Billy told her, nonchalantly.

Then he turned to his own paper.

A paragraph stared up at him, dazing him.

"Lost. Young lady's Golden Garter, supposedly in the vicinity of Chalk Farm. Finder will be rewarded. Apply Miss Lydia Carstairs, 27 Creton Gardens, W."

"Billy, your coffee is going cold," his Aunt reproached him. "Is it something interesting, dear?"

"Oh, a little."

He found he could not eat. What mystery lay behind the Golden Garter? Why, he had found it and returned it, yet here it was advertised for. And it could not possibly have been long in the tube subway, when he found it. That excluded the idea of its having been advertised for prior to his finding it. Adventure! He had always rather longed for it. Now, here it was, and with it was all the absorbing, sorrowful realisation that behind all such mysteries, however criminal, were humanity's pitiful destinies, the threats of ruin, risks to run, and always the tragic illusion that each time was the last, and afterwards they would *go straight.* And *She* was in it! Adventuress, or victim, snare, or the ensnared, she was in it, and with all the chivalrous blood of young knighthood, he was going to try to keep her out of it. Then he recalled that it was Wednesday when he had promised to go to Willard's with Carminetta to drink tea.

When Carminetta arrived, radiant, fresh, wholesome, Billy was on the steps.

"You'll have to go alone, Car," he told her. "I've got some rather important business to attend to. I'd forgotten at the time. Anyhow, Miss Harding,—oh, here she is,—will go with you."

Carminetta paled a little.

Then she said, bravely, "All right, Billy dear."

When their taxi had departed, Billy took another, and was soon speeding in the direction of Creton Gardens. As he stepped out a beggar extended a tin cup towards him gropingly, and murmured, "Blind."

Billy dropped two half-crowns in it. Yes, it was rather a blind sort of world altogether, he mused. Then he hurried on, and noticed, as one does notice irrelevant details, that the doorstep of No. 27 was cleaned once more and that this time it was not white, but yellow. Evidently they changed the colour of the step quite a good deal. In answer to his ring the footman opened the door.

But it was not the same footman.

"Can I see Miss Carstairs?" inquired Billy.

"Out," said the new footman emphatically.

Billy knew he lied.

"I must see her," urged Billy. "It's about a Golden Garter."

He shot the words out at hazard, and had the same astonishment the people who first said "Open Sesame" might have had to find it worked.

"This way," said the new footman.

Billy drew a deep breath as when he had used to take a dive in the Cam,—and followed him.

CHAPTER III

Billy found himself ushered in upon her before he realised that he was to see her just then. He had rather expected an empty room, into which she would come later, when he was prepared to have something sensible ready to say. He felt himself reddening idiotically as she rose from a low stool by the hearth, with, surprise of surprises, a mundane jumper in her hand, on which she was evidently at work. The footman who had ushered him in had gone; at least, he was supposed to have gone, and Billy had supposed he had gone, until he caught her glance on its way to the curtains that hung over the doorway.

"You *feel* a draught?" asked Billy, quickly. He strode to the door and closed it in a lightning second, or almost closed it. There was a yell of pain and fury. Billy opened the door politely and stared into the angry face of the footman. But it immediately became the face of the ordinary immobile footman, and the flunkey was murmuring apologies for having been injured. But for this incident Billy had almost begun to feel that it was an ordinary house, so reassuring had been the appearance of this other room, and Lydia making a jumper so like an ordinary young lady, extraordinary only in the gifts Native had planted in her beauty.

"We thought you had left the room, and Miss Carstairs felt a draught," said Billy. He noticed that it was the left hand the fellow was holding and that there was blood on it.

"I was arranging the portieres," explained the footman.

He departed. Billy closed the door with a snap that was almost angry. It *could* be natural. The fellow could have been arranging the portieres, and yet he could hardly think so.

"Why on earth have you come again?" enquired Miss Carstairs. "Did I not tell I you—oh, bother, I've dropped my stitches. Well, sit down, if you want to, but don't stay, because I've an appointment to keep to-day, and I'm rather pressed for time, Mr.—"

She looked at him questioningly.

Evidently she had forgotten his name in that short time since his previous visit. Or was this pretence, too?

"Durant," said Billy.

He sat down almost aggressively, to remind her that he had come though she had asked him to stay away, supposing him a coward.

"I see that the Golden Garter is still advertised for," said Billy, lighting a cigarette. "Perhaps there are a lot of them! Whose idea was it? Brilliant, call it."

"Don't be an ass, if you can help it," advised Lydia, calmly.

"It was advertised for immediately as I was passing *The Times* office and, of course, they could not know Billy Durant had found it and restored it to its rightful owner."

"Oh," said Billy. Then quickly, "Who told you my name was Billy?"

"You would leave your card," said Lydia, "Most Williams are Billies, aren't they?"

Billy nodded. She had pretended to forget his name, then.

Her pale, clear-cut profile was shown clearly against the dull porphyry green of the fireplace, which was filled with grasses and bulrushes.

It was something at least to be able to sit and stare at her, this pale, mysterious female of the species, who lost a Golden Garter, got him to the house, warned him to keep away, and yet he could not help but feel that she was glad to have him come again. The same mystery, too, who had called someone Jenkins, and said she was sick of the life, and the rest could do as they liked, but she would refuse to do something or other. What? What was it she had refused to do, and then was admonished by Jenkins that she would have to do it, and that it was the last time? Billy pondered her. She lifted her gaze slowly from the jumper and met his. It seemed as though they were challenging each other. Billy's gaze was saying, "Yes, I see you are clever. But I am honest and dogged, which is better." She held her head a little on one side like a terrier he had once kept and said merely:

"Do have some tea."

Billy nodded assent.

She rang a small Swiss cattle-bell, on the table. Someone opened the door.

"Jenkins," she called, "Tea and cakes, muffins and oh, the usual."

"Yes, Miss," answered a docile voice. Billy could have jumped out of his skin. Jenkins! The man she had appealed to in vain to allow her to "leave this life" whatever that meant, and his daytime occupation was to bring in tea and cakes, and answer her humbly, though evidently more than her equal on the evening before. All the blood and thunder tales he had read rushed pell-mell into his head. He realised that had he been an Edgar Allan Poe, with a good chunk of Sherlock Holmes blended, he might have found himself on the threshold of a most fascinating mystery. But the joke was, he was such a fool!

And besides he was less interested in the mystery than in the lady. He was not even concerned about whatever business they carried on, for that was their business or the business of the police, and nothing to do with Billy Durant. Billy sat smoking and trying to think. She had very small, firm-looking hands, he noticed, he wondered if —

"I say," said Billy suddenly, "Would you like to meet a millionaire?"

He watched her keenly.

Quite suddenly he saw the humour of the thing, to introduce her to the Willards. If all was right it would bring her into their set. If it was wrong Willard ought to be able to defend himself against a slip of a girl, Willard, who had thumped fortunes out of steel by thumping steel into men. In the meantime, right or wrong, he would get to see her often, and suddenly Billy realised that not to see her often would leave an emptiness he did not care to face.

"A real millionaire?" she inquired, lazily.

"A real millionaire," Billy told her. "Willard, you know, the steel man."

She nodded disinterestedly.

"Like all steel men, just common flesh and blood," she said thoughtfully. "Yes, I shouldn't mind in the least."

Billy's brain worked rapidly.

There was just time to get to the Willards by tea. He looked at his watch.

"Then come along," he invited. "We've just time to taxi."

She laughed, shaking her head at him.

"Prior appointment," she said lazily. "So sorry. One doesn't meet millionaires every day in the week. Just like my luck. But won't he keep?"

"Oh, rather," said Billy.

Then Jenkins brought in the muffineer, and the cake-stand and went out for the trays.

Billy noticed a hundred things about her to-day, the way she poured out tea, the inflexions of the voice, the calm sort of sadness which in repose settled on the face, which was all vivacity when she was speaking, or thought herself observed. The incongruity of her going about dropping garters annoyed him exceedingly. It was beastly.

"I shan't have to be long," said Miss Carstairs. "I've to go down Palace Green Gardens, at four."

Billy felt to be in the grip of some painful dream.

"How funny!" he said, and laughed boyishly.

Lydia surveyed him.

"I can't see that there's anything funny in going there," she said.

"But, this is the funny part," Billy told her, smiling, "I've to call in that neighbourhood, so we can go together."

He half expected protest.

On the contrary she said, "How lovely!"

Jenkins came in to take away the remains.

"Miss Carstairs will forgive me, but the clock points to a quarter-past three," observed Jenkins, humbly.

"Oh, thanks, Jenkins," said Miss Carstairs. "I had forgotten."

It was all so ordinary, and yet Billy felt that fierce cross-currents were running under it. Who the devil was Jenkins really? Had he not said by the Marble Arch "then we shall be out of it," coupling himself with her?

"I will bring Miss Carstairs' hat and mantle," said Jenkins, bowing his head humbly.

"Thanks, Jenkins," said Miss Carstairs, just as though Jenkins was nothing more than Jenkins. Billy felt suddenly all the fires of jealousy.

"Pardon me," said Billy to Jenkins.

They looked at each other.

Jenkins bowed, smiled and turned away, as Billy took the mantle. Billy suddenly hated his good looks.

Miss Carstairs murmured "thanks" as Billy placed her cloak about her. Quite suddenly he placed his boyish hand on her arm, and as she turned, startled, said simply: "Twice is only twice but I'll think the same when I've seen you a thousand times and I mean to—will you marry me?"

"Hush!" said Miss Carstairs. "Don't be a fool. Hush!"

She gave a terrified glance at the walls as though they had ears.

He would have spoken, but he realised that, after all, there was so little to say. He, Billy Durant, was swept off his feet by a young woman he had seen only twice, living in a house where the footmen accompanied her as friends and equals in the evening. But Lydia Carstairs, still with the same terror stamped on her face, by a silent gesture, urged him to come along with her.

Jenkins let them out.

Jenkins's face was the face of a man who gets so much a year to see nothing, hear nothing, and if possible, think nothing.

"Have a fire in the room, on my return," said Miss Carstairs calmly and with the hauteur it is usual to show to one's dependents.

Jenkins bowed, smiled, and closed the door noiselessly after them.

"Good gracious! My bag!" exclaimed Miss Carstairs.

"I'll go back," Billy told her.

"Oh, don't trouble."

She was up the steps and ringing imperiously. Jenkins opened the door. Two minutes later she came out with the bag, a small vanity affair, black with hand-painted yellow roses on it.

Billy hailed a taxi. They stepped into it, and then, with silence having fallen between them—a speaking silence in which Miss Carstairs had simply held up her hand in protest when he tried to make love to her, an almost tragic movement, though her smile said "Don't be absurd!"—they stepped out and were walking along Palace Green Gardens. Billy's eyes scouted the road. It was almost four o'clock. He took out his watch casually. A few minutes before the hour.

"The trees are beautiful," said Miss Carstairs.

Billy acknowledged the fact.

He noticed a military-looking gentleman coming down the road. But he passed without any sign of recognition.

"And now I will say good-afternoon," said Miss Carstairs.

Billy accepted the mandate.

"My friend has not arrived," said Miss Carstairs. "But I will wait."

Billy took her hand and bowed over it.

"And - some day you can take me to see this Wilson, is it?" inquired Miss Carstairs. "Oh, no, Willard, you said, if he *has* kept!"

He found himself dismissed.

And presently he was walking past the military gentleman. Something made him turn his head before leaving the Gardens. And as he did so there was the military looking gentleman stooping over something on the ground, with his monocle applied to it as though he could not believe his eyes. Billy turned back.

"Excuse me," said Billy politely, "I believe I have lost—"

"Not this, surely," grunted the military gentleman.

He held up, almost with the same amusement which had been Billy's once, a Golden Garter.

"Oh, ahem! I thought it was a cigarette case," said Billy.

"A new kind, if so," said the other.

Then: "Bless my life," ejaculated the military one, "girls evidently carry their addresses on their—"

He paused.

"Exactly so," said Billy.

They stared at each other.

"Well, it's no earthly use to me," said the military one. "What in the world—"

"Leave it, then," suggested Billy. "I should."

Then bearing down upon them, Billy saw an elderly lady.

"Bless my life, she'd never believe me!" said the military one, and stuffed the Garter into his pocket.

"Believe what?" asked Billy.

"That I'd found a thing like that," said he.

"I'll be witness," said Billy smilingly.

"Tut-tut," said the other.

"Good-afternoon," Billy told him.

He walked away and on to the Willards. Late, of course, he would be late. His mind was in a whirl. Dropping Garters was part of some game which was being played in this strange world of London.

And as he plunged into the Willards' tea-party, as he followed the maid, who ushered him into a world of babble, laughter, flowers, and the jingle of teacups, Carminetta's voice came to him, and he got another brain wave.

"Yes, the family jewels of the Durants have gone. Awful, isn't it?"

"What?" yelled Billy.

Carminetta ran to him.

He recalled in a hazy way that the Durant jewels would have gone to his wife, if ever he had one, and that once he had thought sometime of Carminetta, perhaps as Mrs. Billy.

"She's just wired, Billy dear," she said, quite pale. "I think we ought to go at once."

"Oh, must you?" asked Poppy Willard.

She was not in the least what Billy expected her to be, of the fluffy, spoiled type. She was athletic and looked more like a manageress of a shop, saving for her clothes, of course.

"Well, after all," said Billy, "Aunt's jewels can wait."

He knew the hysterical scene they would be plunged into, police visits, smelling salts, the chaotic household, the servants marshalled.

And as he sat down to tea, poured out by the brown hand of Poppy Willard, who looked him over admiringly, he jumped up suddenly.

"Poppy, you will leave pins on the chairs," said Pa Willard reproachfully.

"It—it isn't a pin," said Billy, laughing. "It was an idea!"

Poppy laughed.

"Fancy an idea hurting like that," she drawled. "How many lumps, Mr. Durant? Oh, I say, I'm going to call you Billy."

"Do," said Billy, smiling up at her. "They all do."

"I'm a goner," Poppy told herself. "He's absolutely it!"

Whilst Billy was drinking tea, with the stupendous realisation that the Golden Garter dropped before people was a sign and token of disappearing property, he thought of the military man. To the amazement of the Willards, he suddenly said he would get back home, after all.

"You stay," he urged Carminetta.

She protested.

"I really wish you to stay," said Billy masterfully.

Ill at ease though she was, Carminetta fell in with his evident wish. But it was not homewards Billy posted. He rushed to the office of *The Times,* presented his card, and asked to see the newspaper files for the past six months. Feverishly, he turned the newspapers over, and there at intervals, he found it. The Golden Garter had been advertised for at least four times in six months and on each occasion a robbery had been committed within twenty-four hours of its being advertised for. He took the address of the mansion which had first been robbed, then tore it up in shreds, realising that to go there and ask them to connect the coincidence of the Garter and the missing jewels, if there was anything in it, would—dash it all! *She* was in it, *she* was in it, and he was helpless. Besides, it might be a mere coincidence. And what was it to do with him, anyhow? He went on to his home, to his Aunt's, and as he rang was not prepared for the shock that awaited him. Glory! The footman who had opened the door to him when he took back the Golden Garter faced him, immobile of countenance.

"This is a fever," thought Billy. "Or, I'm going mad."

Aloud he only said: "Where is Ambrose?"

The new footman took his coat and hat.

"Ambrose left, perhaps with the jewels," he said, calmly. "I came from the registry office when the call came for a new one."

It became stranger, and yet more strange.

"Assure me that I am not dreaming," said Billy. "Surely I have seen you at Creton Gardens, you know, when I brought Miss Carstairs'—er—garter back?"

The new footman stared at him.

"Never seen you in my life," he said.

"You're a liar," said Billy.

The footman stared with polite calm and the resignation to be called all things, provided he got his wages.

Billy turned on his heel, and went upstairs to his Aunt's room.

"Oh, Billy darling," wailed his Aunt, from an invalid chair which creaked with her. "The Durant necklace is gone! Billy, it is *you* who have been robbed. They were for your wife."

Billy sat down and tried to be calm amongst it all.

"Well, in any case, I have not got the wife *yet*," he said gently. "And, after all, the jewels are of secondary interest."

She dabbed her nose hysterically.

"But, darling," she urged. "They, oh, Billy, they are all I had to leave you, which is not *entailed*."

She went into violent hysterics again on this confession, and once again Billy felt that he was living an awful dream, having jumped from pale-faced young ladies, who dropped Golden Garters as signals of robberies, to stout ladies, who wailed that everything was entailed.

"But I don't understand," said Billy, when he had quietened his aunt. "I always thought the Durant property was large and—er—I've never worried about it. We've always gone on—er—living."

"Billy, it's all gone!"

With this dramatic avowal his Aunt sat back, and regarded him with the calmness of despair.

"But, it can't be," protested Billy.

"The bankruptcy is pending, Billy," wailed his Aunt. "Billy, you've had a real good time, but it's over. For the Durants have been living beyond their means, staving off with mortgages they hoped to clear off, and now, the net is closing. Six months will see the Durants with nothing, just nothing beyond a miserable four hundred a year, which somehow I shall have to try and live on."

"Poor old girl," said Billy, sympathetically.

"But it's you I'm thinking of," said his Aunt. "Don't you see—?"

Billy ran his hand through his hair.

"I—er—I'll have to do something, certainly," he admitted. "But there's six months, so don't worry, Aunt."

A suspicion was growing in his mind, a suspicion that the jewels had not been stolen, that his Aunt knew where they were, and had removed them so that creditors could not have the heirloom sold. If so, he had been on an entirely wrong tack about the reason for the Golden Garter being dropped. All his theories fell to the ground. It was a pure coincidence that robberies had happened after the dropping of the Garter before, if he could find but that it had missed coming off on one instance. Besides, were not robberies always happening? Still—he determined to know. His Aunt was in almost a collapsing state. He meant to know, not because he cared twopence about the necklace, but because he must know about—about Lydia, and why she went about dropping Golden Garters.

"Aunt," said Billy, bending over his Aunt's chair. "Where are the jewels? You know. I know you know."

She gave him a frantic glance of appeal, and then Billy said, breathing hard, "Don't worry, Aunt. Do as you like. Split them up, tear them from their settings, sell them. Oh, I don't care a damn! But, don't you see, you've set all the machinery of the law working on a wrong trail and someone may suffer for it! And, if it's found out, glory, what a scandal!"

She gave a sobbing, terrified breath, then burst into weak tears.

"I had a glass or two too much of champagne," she said.

"I suppose you got Ambrose to—" hazarded Billy.

Quite suddenly, he felt sick. Lydia's words drifted to his mind.

"Oh, I'm sick of the life, sick of it."

He realised that perhaps all over the world there were people who were sick of their lives, wanting something bigger, better, more honest, more beautiful, from the fag-picker going round Trafalgar Square for old fag-ends to be devilled up again, to the bored idler going from one excess to another to get variety into his or her life. And across his mind flashed the words of a placard he had seen.

"Nine men entombed in burning mine." His life felt suddenly flimsy, worthless, weighed against the heroism of those nine trapped men. Felt ignoble, rotten, vicious, not worth mentioning.

"Aunt, I'm going out," he said impulsively. "Oh, no, not far, just to sit in the garden amongst the sparrows."

But when he was passing along the hall, he faced representatives of Scotland Yard, and saw that his services would be required. His Aunt might go to pieces. What a business! Extravagance, bankruptcy, desperate endeavour to save something out of the wreck, and a big scandal looming up, and away beyond it, like another circle in another hell, Lydia Carstairs, like a beautiful white flower, enmeshed in some flycatching scheme—in which she dropped *Garters*. For what purpose? He could not tell. With a throbbing head, with an inward curse against the life he had lived so long quite happily and blindly, he followed the men of Scotland Yard with their cold, matter-of-fact looks, their note-books, their pencils.

"Why do we live such lives?" Billy was crying inwardly.

Whilst, at that moment, Lydia Carstairs was facing Jenkins: "Yes, Colonel Mallont picked it up. I saw him. You can get to work at once. But remember, it's the last time. I'm taking my holiday now, for I've earned it."

"All right," said Jenkins surprisingly.

"Where are you for?"

"Paris," she told him, and gave him the name of the hotel.

"And if you see any chances there—" suggested Jenkins, imperturbably.

She threw him a frantic look, with white face, and angry eyes.

"Are you going to ask me to *work* on my holidays?" she asked, flame-eyed. "No, I'm going to sit in the sun, and walk in the woods on the banks of the Seine, and find violets, the same violets poor 'Mimi' in Murger's book asked for when she was dying."

"You'll come back?"

Jenkins's question was rather a command.

She gave him a withering glance,

"I shall stick by the lot of you till the time comes for freedom," she told him.

Jenkins laughed.

"You'll have to," he told her, pleasantly, "or you won't be in at the dibs. Then you'll be in the same position you were in when I found you sitting by the Embankment, and ready to add yourself to the numbers the Thames has already taken down to the sea! Or left in the mud, for grappling hooks to dig out. Only, you couldn't do that. You're too afraid of death. You're too modern. Lydia, there's nothing for it but to wait, then you'll get your thousand, and can have your cottage in the country and rear chickens."

He laid his hand on her shoulder.

She stared up at him.

"Yes, I suppose I shall have to wait," she said dully. "I suppose we all have to wait for freedom!"

She went like a flash from the room.

Billy was stupefied. "But Aunt, I couldn't marry Poppy Willard, even if she liked me, which is preposterous."

She gave a gesture of weary despair.

"Well, then, all's lost."

She surveyed Billy.

Then she said: "Besides, why should Poppy be objectionable?"

Billy regarded her grimly.

"Did you ask them here for that?" he demanded.

"Of course not," she snapped. "But it sometimes happens."

"You wished her to approve of me, as the old horse-dealers in the days of the Romans approved of the slaves they bought!" he said. "Well, I'm marrying for love when I do marry. For love. The only thing the world cannot buy, and it buys most everything! And I've seen the woman. I don't believe she's even a lady in your sense of the word. She does odd things, past my comprehension, like dropping Golden Garters—"

Then he stopped.

"What!" almost shrieked his Aunt. "What do *you* know about Golden Garters?"

But before Billy could answer she had collapsed in a heap.

Billy rang for the maid and escaped, to run into the arms of the Chief Inspector.

"You could not tell me if her Ladyship is in any financial difficulties?" enquired that individual. "Or if there has been any untoward demands on her purse lately, could you?"

Billy shook his head.

"Not to my knowledge," he said, and looked the Inspector in the eyes.

"Because there seems to be blackmail mixed up in this," said the Inspector. "There is quite a lot of it going on, at present, the victims selected who are most fearful of scandal, and I found this under the edge of the drawing room carpet."

He held it out to Billy, a dainty note inscribed in a woman's hand, and signed, "Cat." And he saw with stupefaction that on the notepaper was emblazoned a yellow rose—a yellow rose, such as he had seen before.

He burst out laughing suddenly. "Why, 'Cat' is one of our own relatives," he lied splendidly. "I suppose she's asking for money? She's always without. We've helped her out for years. That's no new drain!"

The Inspector's face lost its keen hopefulness.

"An amazing relative who asked for the sum of a thousand at once," he said. 'In any case, I'm keeping this letter. I should like to see this hopeful young lady."

But Billy snatched it suddenly from his hand, ran to the fireplace and pitched it into the fire.

"Carry on your investigations," he said, angrily. "But leave our poor relations out of it. Hang it, you don't think poor Kitty-Cat has got the damned jewels, do you?"

The Inspector took a pinch of snuff.

Billy had destroyed a valuable clue, a literal clue at least, but he could remember the address of the country house in Bucks.

After all, it was his bread and butter to remember such things, and if he got a little tired of it himself, well, in a year or two more there would be freedom, and he was leaving the Yard to keep bees in Surrey. So all men dream, better than they know.

CHAPTER IV

The long, muddled period in which Scotland Yard, hysterics, and his Aunt's appeal to his sense of "duty" had been got over somehow, and here he was in her presence once more, determined to stay, whether welcome or not.

"As you see, I am here again," said Billy, calmly. "You look better."

He had before been told she was in Paris, and now, for some reason, they had allowed him in. For her to pump probably.

She gave him an exasperated look.

"Why on earth did you come again?" she asked wearily. "Haven't you reaped that the place is being watched? Haven't you realised the disgrace it would be if, say, a police raid happened whilst you were here? For us, it doesn't matter much! Jenkins!"

She called, and Jenkins came.

"Bring tea in," she commanded Jenkins.

Jenkins bowed, and left the two sitting by the hearth. Winter seemed to have half turned back. The Spring day was chill and dark. Her hands looked more shadowy than ever. Frail, like china things, almost the blaze of the fire served to turn them into the likeness of blue-veined flesh too delicate for this world's mafficking. Billy and she sat on hassocks, one on each side of the fire, watching the reflected flames dance in the green and white of the polished tiles of the hearth. "Could you not tell me about it?" asked Billy.

She shook her head.

"In three months, we shall have passed from here," she told him, composedly. "You may ring as often as you like, and intrude yourself when you are not wanted. We shall have passed."

Billy answered with sudden intensity. He rose from the hassock, stood with his back to the fire, and looked down on her.

"Do you mean you really wish me to keep away?" he asked, bitterly, revealing himself in that prideless, boyish tone.

She waved her hand. It was an impatient. almost despairing gesture.

"What have you and such as you to do with such as us?" she enquired, fiercely. "You ride on the spray of life, all flashing and rainbow-hued! You float on the top of us, drowning below in the gulfs, and you do not even know we are there, until we rise like vultures and pick off the gold you are gilded with or the jewels you wear. And because I hated you all, hated all you who could pass by on the other side— whilst humanity clawed and ate the dust, as though it was vermin, not flesh of God, left there to die, or rot, or prostitute Itself —because I hated you all, I *joined them.* Still I say, what have I to do with you, or such as you? *Durants.* Land-owners, profiteers, social people, and us—drift-wood, whom no one notices, till we strike you, rising from the deep!"

She had leapt to her feet. They were staring at each other, a little space between them that was wide as the gulf of a class, nay, as the gulf of a world.

Billy tried to seize her hand, fiercely, but she placed hers impulsively behind her.

"No," she said firmly. "No— and No—, and yet, No. I still have nothing to do—nothing to say, to such as you."

Billy saw that she would tell him nothing. Yet it gratified him, made his heart beat more quickly, to realise that she did not withhold whatever was to tell because she distrusted him. Besides, as she had said, in three months it would all be over. Other people would be at this house, and they would have drifted away. One must make the most of it, whilst it lasted, as one did of life.

"And as I told you," she said, in a lower voice, "it would be utter disgrace for a proud Durant to be found amongst *us* if anything did happen."

Billy smiled.

His smile said that he would wish it.

She gave him a look of despair.

"In future you will be refused entrance," she told him.

"Lydia!" protested Billy.

His brain was working rapidly.

There were more ways than one of entering houses where you were getting to be something of a nuisance.

"Very well," he said, with resignation.

She cheered up at his acceptance of his congé.

"That's a good Billy," she said, smiling, and her face lightening into something almost like happiness.

Then Jenkins brought tea in.

47

When he had gone Billy leaned towards her in the fire glow.

"Do you hate me—I mean *us,* now?" he enquired.

She poured out his cup of tea and handed it to him.

"At present," she told him, "I have something to eat, something to wear, and I am getting my own back. No. Not quite so much at present and besides, I realise that you are victims, too. Anyhow, let's forget it, and part friends, you and I, for, after all, neither of us is of our different classes. You are not without heart, and I have energy to think."

She held out her hand, the saucer held in the other. Billy took it.

His own closed upon it.

"You do like me a bit, Lydia?" he asked, smiling, though he felt choked.

"Oh, I shall remember you as a solitary human being amongst a crowd of money-grubbing fiends," she told him. "Yes, you can always think I liked you or, at least, I could have liked you if I'd allowed myself the luxury!"

Without letting her hand go he reached down, and set his cup on the Persian carpet.

"Only one thing, tell me," he said, stiltedly, "why did you drop that Garter for me to pick up?"

"I didn't," she told him. "I threw it down for the be-silkened woman whom I'd shadowed for hours and she missed it, and you became the victim."

Billy recalled now hearing the rustle of a silken petticoat in the tube subway.

"I feel rather a happy victim," said Billy. "Don't please take your hand away yet. After all I didn't make the world, did I? I mean let's believe just for a few hours we are just human beings, who do not prey on each other, fight each other, rob each other, murder each other, in order to exist. Let's believe there is nothing in the world but Love, and Equality,—of course, it's a lie, it's a dream, but let's pretend! Besides, some day it may be true."

"Not yet!" said Lydia, fiercely.

"Not yet," agreed Billy. "But for us, yes, for us, at this moment, it is true. We are equals, and we love."

It did not seem strange to Billy that he should be telling her this, speaking of it so quietly, serenely and relentlessly, saying to a strange woman, whom he had only seen a few times, of whose previous life he had known nothing save what she chose to tell him (which might, after all, be a lie), that they had at this moment equality and love in a world based on neither, but on inequality, and relentless fighting for power, and the possessions that give power. Tomorrow! Why to-morrow they might be enemies! To-morrow she might vanish from his life, still pursuing the strange business which was her profession in life, just as his was that of the idler, the young man his Aunt thought fulfilled all human obligations if he handed cups of tea gracefully, and distinguished himself as a social "asset" in their circle.

Lydia Carstairs was staring at Billy, then, quite suddenly, she snatched her hand from him. The truce was over. He saw it.

And at that moment Jenkins re-entered the room, bringing more cakes.

It seemed to Billy that Lydia flashed him a lightning glance of despair, that her eyes said, quite plainly, "Am I never to have respite, then? Am I forever to have you watching me? Am I to have no rest?"

"Cook sends her apologies. The scones are finished," said Jenkins gravely. "The postman has just brought this, Miss." Lydia took the letter.

Jenkins left the room.

"A visitor," she informed Billy.

"I am going," he reassured her.

He held out his hand a moment or two later, his coat on his arm, and she put her hand in his, for the conventional moment, Jenkins standing by.

"And if you would care to come along to Willard's and meet Carminetta you will find the telephone number on my letter. Do wire me," said Billy.

She nodded.

It seemed to Billy that in Jenkins's presence her eyes always took on the expression of a trapped animal. Or was it only his fevered imagination, for he had certainly found his nerves on edge these past days.

"Good-bye," she said politely.

"Good-bye," echoed Billy, casually.

She went back into the room and Jenkins saw him to the door.

Maliciously Billy found that he could insult Jenkins without hitting him.

"There's a tip, my good fellow," said Billy, patronisingly. "You are a real faithful servant and if ever you're out of a job I'd gladly recommend you to my friends."

He was scarcely prepared for the blaze of absolute hatred which flashed for a moment over the footman's face, then, so rapidly had it passed, he was wondering if *he* had dreamed *that* too, and Jenkins's hand was held out for the silver coin, and Jenkins's well-controlled voice was saying: "Thank you, sir. Shall I help you on with your coat, sir?"

As he ran down the steps, he collided with someone who gave a very English expression of annoyance.

Billy did not show his surprise.

It was the military gentleman, whom he had last seen stooping over the Golden Garter.

"Ah—ah!" said Billy, shaking a warning finger.

Colonel Mallont laughed, a little sheepishly. Then, under the circumstances, he grew confidential. He was properly caught out.

"I thought I'd best bring it back, personally," he said. "Mrs. Mallont does not like strange young ladies writing to me, and would not have understood. Besides, one could scarcely take a thing like that to the Police Station, and there was something so damned odd about it all, seeing there was a photo inside too. I—I thought I'd come and see what *was* behind it all."

Billy repressed a whistle.

"You did as I did," was his comment.

Colonel Mallont gasped.

"Did you—was that your introduction?" he asked.

Billy nodded.

"And you found out—?" asked Mallont eagerly.

"Nothing. Exactly nothing," Billy told him. "You may be luckier."

Mallont nodded.

When Billy looked back Mallont was ringing the bell.

"Poor old fly, who imagines himself a spider," thought Billy.

He walked rapidly back homewards, and just got in in time for dinner.

"There you are!" shouted Cheney Willard at him, across the table. "We are going to the Savoy to-night. Are you coming?"

Billy saw that the millionaire was flushed with champagne. Poppy looked deprecatingly at him, and appealingly to Billy.

"We'll see," Billy answered calmly.

The millionaire got annoyed.

"You must come. Poppy and I can't go to have a two thousand dollar feast all by our lonely little selves!" he protested. "You can ask your friends, any of 'em, everybody welcome, as the missions say! Yep! We'll have a fine old time. Nine o'clock the feed begins. You'll never forget it. It'll be a big (hic)—big thing. Pop'll just have time to rush back to dress, eh, Pop?"

Billy glanced at Poppy Willard.

She looked shamed, and almost on the point of tears.

"All right. We'll all go," he said.

The millionaire stretched his hand across the table.

"Put it there!" he said.

Billy put it.

Poppy Willard's eyes looked gratitude at him.

"You're going, Carminetta?" asked Billy. She was sitting next him, finishing her coffee.

"Of course!" answered Willard.

"Yes, if you want me to, Billy," said Carminetta.

"Billy! The telephone bell's ringing," said his Aunt wearily.

And then Billy heard her voice, dulcet, sweet, travelling along the wires.

Siren! Decoy! Victim!

Whichever of these she was, or all of them, he realised suddenly, as her voice sounded, that she was the world to him, though to her he might be just another fool!

"Yes, this is Billy Durant, speaking," he told her.

"Oh, Billy, if the millionaire has kept," she said, "do introduce me. When shall I come?"

"In two hours here," said Billy. "Put on your prettiest. It's a gala night."

Her laughter tinkled to him over the wires. "I'm looking up the 'Delineator' to see how the aristocracy dress! Bye-bye. I'll be along."

"But Lydia," called Billy.

"I must hurry. And Jenkins is looking daggers," her voice came to him.

Was that a warning that she could stay at the 'phone no longer? Was that a warning that, victim as she was, she was warning him to be prepared for any further development in the Golden Garter scheme? Or was it all bluff, and she and Jenkins hand in glove ready to fleece the lot and get from the world all they could?

Like a man in a dream Billy saw Carminetta into a taxi. She looked rather pathetic and Billy felt a little ashamed of himself. A few short weeks ago and he had been thinking Carminetta held his whole destiny in her girlish hands. He saw the charm of her still, her quiet, shy virtues, the devoted wife she would be, the orthodox and good mother to any children she had. But he saw them far away, far away, for between him and her had swung that which has deluded men through all the ages, a dream beyond, a passion fierce as life and strong as death, a mirage, whose living vision had driven reason to a back seat, and had upset all his concepts of the day before.

"You are looking pale and headachy, Carminetta," he told her. And even as he said it he realised it was scarcely a complimentary thing to say.

"Yes. Life has been rather a hustle lately," she confessed. "The Willards keep awful hours. I don't know when they sleep."

She smiled, and left him to the realisation that she must have been seeing quite a lot of the Willards. He watched the taxi away and dashed in and upstairs to get ready for the "gala" night. Whistling "Night of Stars," he motioned his valet, who got out his evening clothes and spread them out on the bed, satin eider-downed, and the electric light bringing out the polish of the oak, the satiny glint of the wall-paper that had cost ten shillings per foot. He dismissed James, rather astonished to be dismissed, and sitting on the bed, smoked and tried to think about the whole situation. Bankruptcy was hanging over his Aunt's head like a sword! When it fell, if it did, all this would be ended for Billy Durant.

Like Lydia had said of herself and those she was in league with, they the Durants, would have passed, gone down under the tides of the fashionable world which would jog on just the same. In the meantime it was a "gala" night and there was no immediate need to worry. A "gala" night, and she would be there also unwitting of what was to happen to her, also part of the fevered existence in which one flashed along, as she had said, on the rainbow-coloured spray. He looked at himself in the long mirror.

"You are all right, Billy," he told himself.

He tried to see himself with her eyes, as Love has done through the ages.

He wished he had been an honest costermonger and she his mate, for whom he could buy the yearly feathers of triumph. He thought all manner of things which millions had thought before him and the slow hour passed. Then he went downstairs.

"Billy! How splendid, how adorable you look!" said his Aunt.

Billy smiled, a little caustically. Looks! What were they?

Presently they saw Cheney swooping down on them, evidently recovered from his boisterousness of two hours previous.

"How are things going, Aunt? inquired Billy.

"Scotland Yard can't get on the track of the jewels," she told him, fastening her glove.

"Good!" replied Billy in relief.

Then he started.

The footman, who had for some mysterious reason been imported into their household from that of the Lady of the Garter, was coming towards them, a telegram in his hand.

"The boy is waiting, ma'm," he said.

"Tell him to wait."

Billy's Aunt opened the telegram with trembling hands. Billy saw with relief that Carminetta had just arrived and that Willard had turned round and was gone to meet her.

"Oh!" ejaculated Billy's Aunt.

Her face had turned ghastly, ghastly as that of the one who hears, terrible and earth-shaking, the rumbles of the explosion that tumbles all her hopes to pieces, bringing death and disaster.

Billy gripped her elbow to give her courage.

"Let me see, Aunt," he said decisively.

"No, no—"

She stood trying to be dignified, in all the glimmer of dove-coloured satin, which gave her the look of a sleek partridge. Then, under Billy's eye, she held out the shaking telegram. Billy read it in a lightning flash:

"Pay to bearer money owing and all will be well.—SHANEY."

"But it's only another money-demand" said Billy lightly.

"Yes. But this came by the evening post," she almost sobbed, and from the bosom of her evening dress she drew out—the Golden Garter, watching Billy's face.

It had paled, and his eyes had flinched.

"What do you know of it?" she asked with almost the old peremptory manner.

Billy waved a kid glove, nonchalantly.

"Presently, my dear Aunt," he drawled.

"We are—*watched.*" He said it much as though he observed that he needed a match for his cigarette. The footman, the spy, was returning.

"The boy waits, madam," he told his employer.

"Tell him there is no answer," snapped Billy's Aunt.

The colour was coming back into her cheeks, and she was breathing more easily. Billy's careless attitude was giving her reassurance and spirit. The net was certainly closing in on her, but there was still Billy, who did not lose his head.

"Yes, madam."

The footman returned to the door.

"Can't you sack that fellow?" inquired Billy.

"Dismiss him!" ejaculated Billy's Aunt. "Why, he could make a scene and let everybody know."

Billy frowned.

"Who'd believe a footman?" he enquired.

She shook her head despairingly, from side to side. Then she said in a whisper, "Billy, I dare not! *He* has the necklace."

"What?" yelled Billy.

Then he saw the footman returning.

"Why, you could accuse him of the theft," said Billy, swiftly.

"Yes. But the scandal would burst out then, and the creditors would come down. Don't you see?"

Billy did not, but there was not time to say more.

Recklessly he turned to his Aunt and offered her his arm.

"Let's be off," he said.

He could see Willard between Poppy and Carminetta, and Miss Harding had just arrived.

They made an animated group, standing under the hall-chandeliers. Their voices came to him, their laughter, their clear cultured tones, and far away, far away as from another world, dark with sorrows, and wild with hungers, he seemed to hear, like a wail, the voice of Lydia Carstairs.

You float on the top of us, drowning below in the gulf, and do not even know we are there until we rise, like vultures, and pick off the gold you are gilded with or the jewels you wear.

"Let's be off, Durant," said Willard, Impatiently, coming up to them.

"You take the whole bunch," Billy told him. "I'll follow. I'm waiting for a lady." Even as he spoke that much-abused word "lady," which can mean anything or nothing, he recalled grimly that perhaps it would be best, after all, that he should meet the Lady of the Garter quite on his own.

"Anyone I know, Billy dear?" asked his Aunt, a little anxiously. It was not like Billy to spring strange young ladies on their gatherings. Usually he endeavored to escape them in vain.

"Oh—er—Miss Carstairs," he said, watching his Aunt closely.

The name told her nothing.

"Very well, Billy dear. We'll see you later," she told him. Then she went off on Willard's arm, saying, "Isn't my Billy a handsome fellow?"

"A regular pea-nut," agreed Willard, and she realised he had not yet quite fully recovered. It rather profaned her ideas of English high life to hear dear Billy spoken of as a regular pea-nut.

When they had all cleared out Billy paced the

hall. Vaguely he perceived; now, the possibilities of this far-reaching scheme in which well-known people, who were, for various reasons, afraid of scandal, were being used as the pawns who were to give independence to this band of blackmailers. He saw, also, that one of this gang must be someone in "touch" with this "set," someone who knew, intimately, the life behind the glitter. But whom? Someone who, through ill-luck, was trying to preserve his or her place in that social "set" by giving away the secrets of his or her friends—revealing the skeletons in their cupboards *for a price*.

Then the bell rang and the "spy" went to open the door.

Billy would have liked to kick him out, on to the lighted lawn, or preferably to bang him into the geranium vases on each side of the step.

But Diplomacy, that father of Dishonesty, and of Cowardice, said "Wait." It was Lydia who came into the light of the hall.

He loved her, and hated her, more than anything he had loved or hated in his life, as he went forward to meet her.

Moreover, the footman, her spy, was watching the pair of them.

"Sorry to have kept you waiting, Mr. Durant," she said, "I suppose the rest have gone?"

And Billy knew she had played for this, that they should all be gone.

He stood out on the steps, and called the footman to go and hail a taxi. Without word he piloted her down the stone steps, they got into the taxi and were speeding away towards the "gala" night whilst the "footman" decorously departed indoors.

Billy sat opposite to her.

The light and shadows crossed her face, bringing out its exquisite beauty, which the black satin cloak threw into greater glory, as a starless night throws up the splendour of the white moon. She was hatless—wrapless, and upon her dusky hair lay a fillet-band of pearls. The perfume of faint, sad lavender issued from her garments. His enemy! Who had candidly told him she hated the lot of them.

"I am beginning to understand some of this business," said Billy, in a voice sounded cold, even to his own ears. "My Aunt received your telegram just setting out. Was it your telegram? He fancied she started.

"I know nothing about it," she said, as coldly. "You can take my word or leave it. I know nothing about it, I only work my own department."

"And that—" inquired Billy.

"And that *is* my own department," she said cryptically. "After all, as I said, what have I to do with you, or the way you look at things?"

He sat watching her, the lights, the shadows on her face. Suddenly they were flung upon each other; she gave a little cry of girlish terror just as Carminetta would have done.

Billy shouted to the driver.

"A skid!" called that man, reassuringly. "A narrow shave. We touched the kerb."

They went on again, but not before Billy had realised, with beating heart, that she had cried out, like any other girl, like Carminetta would have done, that she was flesh and blood, born of the earth, not a pale dream, with eyes of beauty. Flesh and blood, human with humanity's hopes and fears and therefore attainable. He seemed to be smothering in the pleasure of having touched her, for a lightning moment.

She was staring at him, wondering evidently what he would say next.

"You remember what I said once before," said Billy. "I say it again. I—"

She held up her hand with the little despairing gesture he remembered so well. "Don't say it," she said shuddering. "Don't! I have heard men say they *love* so often I am sick of it! Sick to death of it! If you want to *please* me, hate me. It would be a—a change!"

The taxi stopped.

They were at the end of the ride, which might perhaps be their last ride.

He helped her out!

Gala night!

It stretched before them, unexplored, glittering, empty, tinsel in its sham. The doors of the Savoy flung open. Beauty, artificial, yet so near to life one could think it real, blossomed out at them and she took his arm and they walked in upon it.

"Mr. Willard's party is in the furthest room, sir," a waiter told Billy in answer to his enquiries.

They followed him.

Billy heard her give a quick breath.

"Isn't it queer," she asked smiling up into his face, "One dreams of this kind of thing and then finds the glamour gone before one touches it! I was wondering if it was worth it!"

"Worth what?" enquired Billy.

"Oh, never mind," she said. Then the waiter paused at the door of the room engaged by Willard.

"Swim in," shouted Willard.

Lydia and Billy were both surprised. They had never expected this. Almost for a moment one could think it really as beautiful as life, so faithfully had art reproduced Nature. And the tinkle of a guitar, playing jazz, came to them over the room, which had been turned into Venice. That was the only jarring note.

CHAPTER V

"Oh!" Again Billy Durant heard Lydia Carstairs draw a deep breath. It was beyond imagination, evidently. Her hand rested on his sleeve. She looked more like a wondering child transplanted into some fairyland of dreams which had never come true than an adventuress. Billy realised bitterly that she could be both.

"The floor has been lowered," he explained to her. "They can do wonderful things at the Savoy."

"Yes."

She stared at it all, in its first glamour, bluey waters in which cunningly placed lights on the walls gave long quivering streams of reflected radiance. Colour! It blazed from the water to the roof, where the dim lights suggested stars and a big one the glory of the moon, and there were the trembling reflections of the lighted gondolas in the water, too. Garlands of flowers on the walls, great sprays of mimosa. One half expected windows opening, and to see some passionate Italian face peering out into the witchery of a star-lit night, ears eager to catch a drifting serenade. It caught at Billy, too. There was magic in it in which one drifted, drifted, drifted in the spirit of carnival, and cared nothing for the morrow.

His hand closed on the one on his sleeve, "You will come into my gondola," he almost begged.

She roused as from some lotus-spell of enchantment.

"I—I have not come purely on a pleasure trip," she told him.

"Lydia!" he beseeched suddenly. "Drop this life. Whatever it is. I worship you."

She stared up at him, a slightly mocking smile on her face, which faded under the earnest intensity of his look. Then she said, without looking at him, "Impossible, Billy. Don't spoil tonight."

She looked at him again, and he was conscious of the sad wisdom in her eyes.

"There's Carminetta, at least I think it's the girl you've told me of, over there. She's very pretty. Suppose we go in her gondola?"

"No."

Billy breathed it swiftly.

"Just you and I," he begged.

"For part of the evening," she consented, surrendering suddenly.

Billy had never felt so deliriously happy in his life. Already a gondola was coming to the step for them, brought by Willard, who had a carnival hat on his head, Willard who shouted "Ah! Youth and Beauty! This is your lady friend?"

He stood up in the gondola and took off his hat, sweeping it to his feet, and looked absurd, in his genial ugliness.

"Two's company, Willard," said Billy pointedly.

Willard grinned.

"Step in, you fool. Don't I know it?" he asked. "I'll row you up to Miss Dawson's boat, gondola, I mean, and leave you. The feast is coming in shortly. So arrange yourselves."

His eyes took keen stock of Lydia Carstairs.

"That, I presume, is your Aunt?" asked Lydia, pensively, trailing her hand in the water, as she seated herself.

Billy nodded.

His Aunt was in a gondola with Miss Harding and a gentleman he could not recognise. He wished to forget them, to forget the whole world.

"Miss Dawson! Yep! I'm here again," said Willard, bumping the gondola into the one where she sat, drifting, a lonely occupant, in a white dress, with a garland of Savoy-supplied flowers in her hair.

"So, I see," laughed Carminetta.

She flashed a rapid glance at Lydia and Billy.

"Miss Carstairs, a friend of mine, Carminetta," said Billy, standing up. They surveyed each other from the two boats, rival queens of opposite worlds, one born to ease and comfort, the other drifted up from the gulfs, and they smiled, with feminine wisdom.

Then Willard sprang into Carminetta's gondola, with its flower-wreathed prow, and they glided away, and Poppy Willard's voice, singing a Canadian boat-song, a song of those who go down to the rapids, rose over the laughter and talk.

"What are you thinking of?" asked Billy.

He tossed her an orange-coloured cushion, silk, filled with down, for her delightful head to lean against, and make a picture all for him to remember till the crack of doom.

"Contrasts," said Lydia, letting her hand trail through the water. "Just contrasts. Here's a guitar. Can you play?"

"Just a little," said Billy. "But not when I'm rowing."

So he let the oars rest, and they drifted, drifted through the bluey waters, and finally grated against one of the islets, planted with the mimosa which dangled over their heads.

The rest were moving about restlessly. They alone were still, and Billy slid down into the bottom of the gondola, and played, and sang, whilst she smiled upon him and they could almost believe that had nothing at all to do with the real world. He was lilting "Night of Stars," and she was listening with an almost girlish smile, and suddenly, he said entreatingly, breaking off, "Marry me, Lydia. Do! and I'll cut the whole lot!"

"Hush!" she breathed in a terrified whisper.

"Evening, Miss Carstairs," came a voice that made Billy jump. There, in the glory of evening suit, was Jenkins with Billy's Aunt in tow.

"Good evening," said Lydia.

Jenkins turned to the lady in the gondola. Even in the dim, diffused light, Billy saw his Aunt's face would have been pale if she had not re-rouged.

"Lady Durant, my sister," said Jenkins. And Billy saw that Jenkins, Jenkins was the master-mind, and had got the whip hand.

"Charmed to meet you," said Billy's Aunt, languidly. Hysterical as she was, Billy could not but applaud her courage now, though he realised it might only be the courage of despair.

Lydia and Lady Durant shook hands over the side of the gondolas. Lady Durant's touch cold. Lydia's was warm and steady.

"I have just proposed to your sister," said Billy. "I wish you could persuade her to listen to me."

He caught a look of dismay on Lydia's face, and Jenkins was laughing, saying, with an affectionate glance at her, "I'll do my best," whilst Lady Durant, with a glance of frozen horror, drifted away, drifted, in Jenkins's gondola, through the nightmare of a world that was turning to dust and ashes.

"Oh! you shouldn't have done that!" said Lydia. "You know Jenkins is only my footman."

"You must tell me nothing," said Billy. "Nothing. What I said stands. I'll marry you."

Lydia Carstairs slowly unclasped her cloak. The golden dress she had flowered out on each side of her.

She was staring at Billy, like one who sees before her either confession or a degradation she cannot face, a last hypocrisy before which her soul cries out, "Spare me this."

"Look!" she told him, leaning forwards. "Look!"

Her voice was quite steady.

"I am all eyes," Billy told her. Then he rubbed his hand across his eyes, and looked again. Upon her neck, glittering with all its fire of precious stones, was the Durant necklace.

Billy glanced around.

"Cover it up," he urged. "Carminetta would recognise it! I suppose you are the bearer to whom the thousand has to be paid."

She nodded, calm, pale.

"Yes. I am the Cat," she told him. "I get the chestnuts out of the fire."

She drew her cloak about her.

Carminetta's gondola passed with Willard, singing a coon song in nasal tones, happy at Carminetta's laughing at him. There was a hustle of the gondolas all together, and the feast came in, a door opening to let a gondola through, with the waiters dressed as gondoliers, champagne in tow, and delicate foods, and everyone was eating, having food loaded into their gondolas. The lights came up showing all the "rainbow-coloured spray" of civilisation. Whilst underneath—Billy shuddered at the thought.

Jenkins was telling Club tales to the manner born. There were bursts of merriment all about him, and Billy was saying to Lydia "Eat," and, thus admonished, she was eating with this new terror hanging over her head.

"My sister," announced Jenkins, suddenly, "has become engaged to Mr. Durant. That is the funniest story I know."

Billy's heart gave a great leap. He saw Lydia blanch and redden, and then there was a chorus of laughter and congratulation, to which he found himself standing up, responding to toasts and noticing, as one notices minor details in moments of great excitement, the frozen horror of his Aunt's face which was reflected in Lydia's. He saw Carminetta valiantly biting a sandwich. She was trying to smile, and the smile hurt him a little.

Finally they all went off again. Laughter and the singing grew louder, and Willard became master of the ceremonies. More champagne was brought by the gondoliers and Billy, taking out his watch, said in tones of unbelief, "It's twelve o'clock, Lydia."

He looked at her possessively.

She leaned forward.

"That—that scene was a joke," she said, angrily. "You must explain it as such. Just a mad joke in a mad night. Look at them! Do you mean to tell me any of these people are acting like sane human beings?"

"That was an announcement of our engagement," said Billy, grimly. "I want you, Lydia. I don't care, whence, where, what you have done. I want you. You know you do care a little bit."

"You are mad all of you," she told him almost passionately. "I shall deny, deny."

Almost he thought she was going to break down and cry, like human flesh and blood.

"You don't like me, then?" he enquired.

He was standing in the gondola looking down on her.

She flashed him a despairing glance.

"Oh, Billy, that's why," she said, "that's why."

He sped the gondola under the mimosa and seized her hands to kiss them, the hands of the Cat, whatever that term connoted, apart from what he guessed.

She placed them behind her.

"Oh, no, Billy," she said, "I'll—write you. I'll explain. I'll—I'm make a clean breast of it. You don't understand the position I'm in."

"I—Jenkins—I mean Harvey, no, I'll have to write it," she said in distress. "I can be clearer when it's written. It's so unbelievable, so awful that this position should have arisen. Everything was going so gloriously. Billy, take the gondola up to your Aunt's."

Billy obeyed.

He understood so little, excepting that odious word "Blackmail," and that his Aunt was in their grip, understood so little, except that he was going to lift her out. of this life, of which, he had heard her say herself, she was sick to death. He thought of a ranch out somewhere away from all this mad glitter, where a man could live a man's life and a woman could be—a woman, and there were wide, clear skies, and a rough freedom, and honest affection.

"Lydia wished to be in with you," said Billy, simply. "By the way, it's midnight."

"Early yet," said Jenkins.

Then Willard and Carminetta came past them. Carminetta's cheeks were flushed. Her first champagne, Billy guessed, with a cry against it in his heart. Yes, Lydia was right. They were mad.

And Willard, standing up unsteadily in the gondola, was urging Carminetta to stand up also.

"We are also—are engaged," said Willard, swaying with the gondola. "Just happened now. I'm, I'm overwhelmed. Miss Dawson and I, that is Carminetta, have, as your magazines say, arranged, yes, arranged is the word, a match."

Billy stared at his Aunt, who was sitting stiffly in her seat. He saw a look of unutterable relief, of wild hope, steal into her face, and realised she saw hope, hope of escape; from Jenkins and his gang, for was not her dear young friend, Carminetta, engaged to a millionaire?

Jenkins's voice came to them, steady and cool.

"Lady Durant has fainted, I think," he said.

Amidst all the confusion Billy saw the party break up. Lilian Harding and Poppy Willard got Lady Durant away and Carminetta, with Lydia, was in Billy's charge. His head was in a whirl as he saw Lydia go off in the taxi. Carminetta ran up the steps with him to see his Aunt, before going home. And a little later, as he knocked on the door of his Aunt's bedroom, walking in, as no one answered his knock, he saw the two women, Lady Durant grasping Carminetta's hand. She was saying in a sob-shaken voice, "You'll do that for me, dear, won't you? For my sake and Billy's? Won't you? Just a few thousands which will be nothing to Willard. Otherwise there's nothing but prussic acid!"

Billy stole out of the room.

So!

Carminetta, out of pique, was engaged to Willard and must bleed him to save her friend.

"What a life!" he ejaculated, leaning his head against the window-frame. He saw the stars. She might be looking on them, he thought.

But he was wrong.

Lydia was facing Jenkins.

Both were white to the lips.

"How dare you?" she asked him, vehemently. "How dare you trap me to such an extent. You know I won't do it. How can I? Besides, don't you see that Dawson girl will get all you want. Lady Durant can have help now and you'll get the money. What more do you want? You know I can't marry that boy, you know I can't. What's the game?"

"Be quiet, Lydia," said Jenkins.

She sat down, her hands on her lap, regarding him wearily.

"Will you listen?" said Jenkins.

She nodded.

"There can't be any need to marry him. You can dodge out of it, but the engagement will give wonderful possibilities, the reception, and all that, then we can scoot, at the first great coup, and have done with it."

She closed her eyes, like one too weary to think any more.

"But supposing he urges early marriage?" she asked.

"So much the better," said Jenkins.

"Think! Why, if the Willards are at the reception of the engaged couple there'll be at least two thousand pounds of jewels on Poppy Willard, and Carminetta would brush Willard up for Lady Durant's sub."

She rose wearily, and threw off her cloak. Then she unfastened the Durant necklace which had been worn by the proudest of the proud.

"Take it," she told Jenkins.

He held it in one hand.

"You are most adorable, Lydia," he told her.

She gave him a glance of scorn.

"Fie! Lydia! Looking like a fury at your husband," he said.

His gaze rested on her face. He placed his arm round her waist.

"You do like me a bit," he mocked.

So! He had heard that too!

Her dark eyes rested on him.

"Like poison," she cried contemptuously.

Jenkins still kept his grip.

Slowly his face came nearer hers, which was white and disgusted.

"Kiss me, and I'll pitch the Durant necklace on the tiles," she told him in a low voice, and snatched the necklace.

He released her.

"Not worth it, not for a kiss, Lydia," he told her practically. "After all, you did marry me."

"Yes, to get the prospect of a secure life. And it has been secure! Oh, yes, it has been secure. I'd better have gone over the parapet!"

She threw the necklace at him, suddenly, a very Cat, and flung from the room, Jenkins just managed to catch it. Pale and sweating with fright, he took it to its case. Then he slowly mounted the stairs.

"Are you in there, Cat?" he asked at the door.

There was no answer.

He tried the door. Locked and bolted.

"Love locked out," quoted Jenkins calmly. "Lydia! If I thought you cared twopence for Durant, I'd,—I think I'd murder you."

Her voice came to him, muffled.

"After all, I didn't promise to *love* you," she taunted.

Jenkins took a flying kick at the door.

Someone came running up. It was the "footman" who had taken his place.

"Kindly remember, sir, we are living in a very respectable neighbourhood," he said, punctiliously.

Jenkins stared at him.

Then their laughter broke out unanimously.

"Yes. We must not bring down the value of the property," he mocked, "or get turned out. But the Cat is extremely trying. After all, she's my wife."

The other nudged him.

"She's been very useful. Treat her as you like afterwards," he said. "Let's make good and finish. They're getting on the trail."

Jenkins nodded. They went downstairs and dined.

Whilst Lydia sat, later, trying to write it, only—she could not. She hoped Billy would think she had been hysterical! Hysterical! She laughed, suddenly! She pushed the paper away irritably. It was impossible to write it or say it. Besides it could be termed "blowing the gaff."

CHAPTER VI

"The Cat" and "Slimmy" sat in a third-rate restaurant, this being Slimmy's choice. They surveyed each other with curiosity.

"How's your cough, Jim?" asked the Cat, with un-cat-like sympathy. "I believe you look a little better. Cheer up! You'll soon be out of Shaney's grip and you'll brighten up like an old hat in an April shower."

Slimmy struggled with his cough, triumphed over a rising burst of it, and his dull, sad gaze brightened a little.

"I believe I've not been quite as bad this last week or two," admitted Sliimmy.

"But when the fogs come down it'll be hell."

"Oh, it's a sharp, bad run just for a bit, now," said Lydia. "Then, maybe we'll both be out of it." Her tone told of almost despairing hope.

"The worst of it is," said Slimmy, moodily, "this cough could get me nabbed. It sounds so when all's quiet as a grave. I'm full of chlorodynes, ram-jammed full of 'em!?"

Lydia said nothing.

But her gaze was full of all the sympathy she found it difficult to put into words. Besides, she was rather afraid of men. They were so awful, mostly animals, she had sometimes thought, or perhaps it was that she had been unlucky, because Shaney had taught her all she knew of men.

"I reckon you're the unhappiest of us two," said Slimmy, thoughtfully."Shaney bagged you, for life an' all. Whatever made you do it?"

She answered him, eating as she answered.

"Fate!" she told Slimmy.

"Fate be hanged," retorted Slimmy. "There ain't no such thing. We makes us fate, we does, an' we unmakes it every day. It's a wonderful thing, life! Blast me cough!"

He looked deprecatingly at her.

He knew he looked a miserable weed, shaking in that gust of coughing and in his dreams, for even Slimmy dreamed better than he knew; he was always rather an improvement on the actual fact and he whom Shaney had scornfully dubbed "The Magic Key," on account of his puny body, was a knight in shining armour in his dreams, his wonderful dreams, sometimes killing Shaney, and giving her her liberty, with the rope round his neck, sometimes betraying Shaney, and being killed by him and waking, screaming with fear, and upsetting his landlady, sometimes marrying her, Shaney having killed himself, very conveniently; but the last dream always made him most sad because, he knew, after all, Slimmy marrying her would be as rotten as Shaney having married her.

"So the latest is you're to marry into the English aristocracy," said Slimmy as soon as he got his breath.

Lydia nodded.

"There it is!" she told him, unconcernedly, fishing the paragraph from her bag.

Slimmy took it.

"Don't—grease it, Slimmy," she said, almost irritably.

He looked at her in surprise.

"Nice bloke?" he asked.

"H'm! Not too bad," she acknowledged.

Slimmy looked at her.

"Poor devil!" was his sole comment.

"However, he'll waken up before the wedding bells ring and they sing "The voice that breathed o'er Eden.'"

"Don't let's talk about it," said Lydia, shortly. "It's not very palatable, Jim. Anyhow, it's the last of cheating. We've agreed to break up, after."

"And then you and Shaney will keep chickens," scoffed Slimmy. "I can see you keeping chickens, but not Shaney."

She leaned her chin on her hands, elbows on the table's edge where it was not greasy, and looked at Slimmy, without saying a word.

"So you'll not keep chickens with Shaney?" gurgled Slimmy. "You're going to slip him?"

"I—I'd rather commit suicide than keep chickens, with Shaney," she said, calmly.

Slimmy sat bolt upright.

Now he knew he would get nightmares.

His nail-bitten hand stole across the table, and touched hers appealingly, dejectedly, with the compassion of the unfortunate, and the mournfulness of the outcast.

"Don't do nothing of the kind," he urged, intensely. "Don't do nothing of the kind, pal."

And suddenly she was almost crying over her tea-cup, the thick, ugly pot made to stand all knocks and not break, the poor pot that held a lot, the useful article that served the useful, and Slimmy was wondering what had done it, for she had shown hitherto a mettle like a wild cat's. Suddenly his eyes took on the momentary brilliance Slimmy's eyes occasionally showed, burning black in his puny face, when he got an "idear."

"You ain't in love with that bloke, are you?" he enquired.

She lifted an indignant face.

"Love!" she ejaculated bitterly. "Slimmy, I've had enough love to last ten lifetimes. Come on. Eat up. And let's go."

"I'm glad," said Slimmy, "to be corrected. Love makes an awful mess o' things, an' blows the gaff oftener nor revenge. I only wondered what made your eyes water."

They passed out into the street, took a taxi, and discussed strict business. And amongst the talk the name of Mallont appeared quite frequently.

"You mustn't dare get in till you see the advert, Jim," she warned him. "And to be doubly sure, walk past the house, and notice the colour of the step. It is quite possible that other mistakes could happen like that last week and, of course, it, was explained from the office how it happened, but it could have been serious."

Slimmy nodded thoughtfully. It could. He had almost been caught.

Lydia looked at her wrist-watch.

"And now I'll have to leave you, Jim," she told him. "I'm to go on to my fiance's. Be good.

And don't chlorodyne too much, after all, you'll perhaps be in Canada before the fogs come. I'll speed up the engagement reception, then you'll be through with it soon. Shaney will let you have a plan of the house. And Ginger is in possession. So it'll be easy."

They were sitting close together, so that she could talk into his ear, and the pulsations of the taxi drowned the sound of their voices to the driver.

"Good-bye," said Slimmy.

"Good-bye," Lydia answered.

When the taxi stopped and she got out, Slimmy could have laughed, to see her so ostensibly an orthodox young lady going to tea to the house of her fiance. But laughing set him off coughing, so he did not give way to it. Whilst Slimmy, it was in the irony of things that Slimmy, so little to look at, knew that had he been the most fortunate being alive and the worthiest, would have picked her up from the gutter of hell itself and placed her in equality at his side.

***

"Ginger" answered her ring. He was certainly "in possession." He managed to say one word to her which put her on her guard and no more.

"Beaks," his lips had told her silently, as he stood face to face with her.

"Is Billy in?" she was asking Lady Durant, who had come from the drawing-room.

"Yes. He's waiting to take you out," she said, frostily, "all impatience." She smiled stiffly, endeavouring to keen the vinegar from her tones.

"Just at present I wish him to stay until—the police have gone."

"Police!" ejaculated Lydia with simulated horror in her voice. She had just seen the Inspector entering the hall. She was playing the part of the terrified young lady.

Lady Durant gave a weary gesture.

"Yes, Lydia dear," she said, "unfortunately my necklace has not yet been traced."

"Oh, that again!" said Lydia sympathetically. "Poor dear!"

She leaned forward and kissed Lady Durant as these people did peck at each other, even whilst detesting each other. Then she felt irritably that it was, after all, rather a mean revenge.

Lady Durant turned and went to talk to the Inspector they were both trying to delude.

"Billy!" said Lydia.

She had turned into the fire-lit drawing-room where he was sitting. He jumped up at her entry and came striding towards her as though an eternity had passed since the night at the Savoy. She had been able to put him off seeing her for almost a week on the plea of a cold.

His lips were coming near her cheeks. She lifted a gloved hand, tapping his face playfully.

"Not hygienic, Billy dear," she laughed. "I've had flu."

She pushed him away, and went to sit down in a chair by the fire. It was not an assumed weariness. Quite suddenly, life seemed too much for her, a something she had set out to manage so high-spiritedly, so reliantly, so innocent-heartedly— and which threatened to manage her, the Cat.

His disappointment struck at her like a blow. On one thing she was determined. He should never have to remember, wishing to kick himself, that he had not only loved Shaney's victim, but kissed Shaney's wife, kissed the deluding partner of Shaney's guilt and Shaney's folly, which was ever menacing them all by its over-insulting condition to succeed beyond success.

She had a vague and wistful idea that, out of the muddle of it all, it would be rather great to leave him with only the memory of what might have been had life been kinder and leaving him to kiss Carminetta with lips that had nothing more passionate on them than a faint regret.

A lesser man, she recognised, would have pushed away her evident desire to avoid being kissed.

Billy drew a hassock, sat down a short distance from her, and opened his cigarette case.

"Have one?" he queried.

She nodded, accepting it, and wondering if Ginger had really got the full plan of the house ready.

"It's most comfortable indoors, this afternoon, Billy," she told him.

"I thought——he began, disappointedly.

"Yes?"

He looked at her through their curling cloud of cigarette smoke.

"I thought it would have been rather nice to go on the river," he hazarded. "I'm really quite an expert oarsman."

"Clever boy!" she told him. Billy's brow clouded.

"Oh, I've never been noted for cleverness," he

said, "but I'm rather honest, Lydia. Don't you think you owe it to me?"

Then he paused.

Lady Durant's voice, rather high-pitched, was saying to the Inspector, "But it's preposterous that it can't be found. What are the police doing?"

And the Inspector's voice came back, "We are doing all we possibly can, madam. We have come to the conclusion that this is a very clever affair, and not an ordinary case at all."

Then the door closed behind him.

Lady Durant sailed into the drawing room. She was almost shaking with hysteria and anger.

"So you've got my nephew in your toils, you've got my necklace, you've protected yourself behind me and made it impossible for me to do anything and I suppose you can say you've won!"

Lydia opened her bag.

"I've brought it back," she told Lady Durant.

"And I suppose when you've done with him you'll return Billy!" said Lady Durant.

Billy jumped up.

"No," he said, in a low, steady voice, "she won't return me. I refuse to be returned. Do you hear, Lydia?"

"A *thief*" said Lady Durant. "A thief—and a *Durant*! It's abominable—outrageous—beyond imagination."

Lydia sat quietly. .

"You won't return me, will you, Lydia?" asked Billy, in the same low, steady voice, ignoring his Aunt.

"A thief!" repeated Lady Durant. Her eyes half closed in the anguish of it.

Lydia said nothing.

She was staring at the carpet. It was rather like one of their old carpets at home before she had known anything about thieves, either legal or otherwise.

"After all, the Durants pinched all their land during the rise of manufacturing," she said, calmly.

"Don't defend yourself!" said Lady Durant. "Don't. You are a thief and that's enough."

She went from the room, swaying as she walked, and Lydia sat staring at the carpet, starting a little as Lady Durant whirled back into the room with: "I'm arranging the reception in a month, and you can remove your spy from my house."

Lydia nodded.

Then the door closed behind Lady Durant with a bang not unlike that an irate servant-maid might give, for, after all, she was only human.

"You, you won't return me, Lydia, will you?" persisted Billy, smiling. He looked a little strange and un-Billyish.

"Well, it's scarcely likely, is it?" she asked, and the sudden happiness which flashed into his face gave her a feeling of nervousness—quite uncanny and unusual in Shaney's wife. She set herself out to please him, to entertain him, with a sudden sense of owing him something, wishing to leave him something worth stirring over in his memory, when he had come through all this sordid muddle and only recalled her dimly and far off as a victim, as he had been a victim.

"You do think I'm rather nice, don't you?" asked Billy boyishly.

He was sitting cross-legged like a tailor, at her feet; and looking up at her.

"Glorious!" she told him, playing up to him. They both laughed. Then he got up suddenly, boyishly, and took her hat off, and went and sat down again.

"The fire, that's glorious, too," she said. And away across her memory trailed the shuddering recollection of an hour when she had felt she could sell her soul for the warmth of a fire, for the heat from the "black diamonds" brought up from the earth's breast to warm humanity.

Billy basked in the sunshine of her calm smile, her full attention. Once he had made a boyish manoeuvre to beat down her opposition to his kissing her, looking at her with puzzled eyes.

"Oh, I don't take things," he protested.

"You do!" she accused him, lightly.

"You take all and give nothing. All the lot of you."

And at last the afternoon was over and she was free—free to rush away.

She was feeling quite worn and unaccountably depressed, considering that in a month all would be over.

The sprat of Lady Durant's necklace was rendered up to catch the mackerel.

"Oh, don't ask me any questions, now," she said to Shaney as she rushed past him. "The reception's in a month. Leave me alone."

Shaney was sometimes diplomatic. But an hour later he went and knocked at the door of her room.

"Lydia!" he said. "Open the door. Something awful has happened."

She opened it and stared half-believingly into his face. Then she saw its colour. Shaney was ashen, his eyes blazing.

"That advert. did not get in by mistake," he told Lydia. "It's in again and we've not sent it. Who's ratting? Why, Slimmy may blunder and walk into a trap and we with him!"

They stared at each other.

"I asked Slimmy always to walk past the house and notice the other code," she said. "So that's all right. I've warned him."

"But who?" asked Shaney, viciously. "Who?"

She shook her head.

It was a mystery.

"Do you think Mallont is cuter than we know?" asked Shaney, thoughtfully.

"Mallont is an ass," Lydia answered shortly.

She looked so superb, standing there, her hand on the edge of the door, her beauty flowering on the twilight of the landing like a scented white flower, that Shaney made a grab at her. Just as he had once grabbed at her, panic-stricken with terror, in the mist of a London night, holding her hand in a grip like a vice and asking, "What is your hand doing in my pocket?" Hunger, half-death had answered him from her face, as he had dragged her to the light of a lamp. He had believed her confession that it was the first time she had stolen, and she had been stealing to save herself from a worse crime, another night outside at the mercy of her terror, men. A country girl, who knew nothing about hostels for stranded women and who had starved three days and slept out three nights, after having her own small wealth stolen, and faced with all the ignorant horrors of a strange city.

"No, you don't, Shaney," she told him, fiercely. They were struggling together when the footman ran up.

"Oh, leave your damned love-making," said the footman irately. "Old Mallont's at the door. You'll have plenty of time to make love, Shaney, when you get amongst the chickens and live the simple life. Come on. I've seen him through the window. He's as drunk as a lord."

Shaney released Lydia's hand.

"And you," said Shaney to her, "come down. You can get to know all the ins and outs of his affairs now. Business before pleasure."

She straightened her hair, refreshed her face, stood for a moment gathering herself together, trying to think. But one thought beat in her brain like a deep minor chord. She tried not to listen to it, but still heard its surge.

"If ever he does get into the room— I shall kill him."

Whilst Billy was staring into the fire which, as its embers fell, made a picture of a ranch, far out, under a wide sky, where Spring came freshly after every storm, and life for her could begin all over again.

"Ah, there you are, Colonel, said Lydia. "How are you ? "

"Excellent," she was informed. "Excellent, my dear young lady. Let me sit down."

"Jenkins, tea," called Lydia.

The Colonel waved his hand, erratically, deprecatingly.

"My dear young lady, I came to see you, not drink tea," said the Colonel. "Fact is, I rather,— rather think I'd like you to meet my wife. She's jealous— frightfully so—ridiculously so. But I've told her all about you, and we're giving a little party, and I said I'd ask you to drop in. Have you?"

He looked round for the matches.

Lydia lit his wavering cigarette. There really were times when she felt it would be heaven never to see a man again! Only there were heroes amongst them, and useful people, and just a few like Slimmy and Billy: one in the dregs of life's cup, one amongst the bubbles at the top, neither knowing the other but saving her faith, which Shaney had almost destroyed.

CHAPTER VII

She had promised to meet Billy at three, at three exactly, rain or shine, beside the stone steps around a certain old monument where the city flower-sellers stand, unwitting of the history of the spot, too engrossed in the history of their own struggle to live, to read history. She saw Billy, as she came along unhurriedly, talking to one of the flower-girls, as he bought one of the earliest roses. And an old line of poetry she had been smacked for learning out of Herrick long ago—oh, long ago!—flitted into her mind:

"Gather ye rose-buds whilst ye may,
For time is still a-flying ..."

Yes. It was certainly flying.

The flower-girl was still looking after Billy. Just as in days to come perhaps *she* would still be looking after him from a fettered life with Shaney and Shaney's chickens.

"Gather ye rose-buds whilst ye may."

The voice of the wise poet singing to Youth!

"Here on time," she told Billy.

"Wonderful," said Billy, smiling.

She smiled also, almost feeling the smile, almost like a reflection of his happiness.

"And I thought," said Billy, "we'd go to Epping. It's quiet there and beautiful."

"Oh, let's go to the Tate Gallery," she inveigled him.

"But just for once to please me—Epping," asked Billy, I—we're always amongst crowds. You see, I'm sure there are things we ought to talk over and it's so quiet and beautiful, far from the madding crowd sort of thing, there. Do you never want to please me, Lydia?"

"Oh, Lord, yes," she said, laughing.

She watched the throng for a lightning second or two.

"Epping then," she agreed.

So to Epping they went. They were soon speeding along to the quiet, the dreaded.

"Mind you, Billy," she warned him, as they plunged into the cool green of the Forest, "I must be back early.'

Billy assented.

"Soon I shall have you to myself," he told her. "Really, Lydia, I don't know how to get the days over. Oh, the reception is on Wednesday night, seven prompt. *The Dandover* is coming."

They went deeper into the sylvan beauty of the Forest. The beeches made a world of their own. The sun glinted amongst them, and where they had to lift the boughs, to clear their passage with unbent heads, sparrows—almost like dream sparrows, so unafraid, so confident—hopped at their feet on the bright grass. They sat down on a sunny slope, where a break in the beeches overhead showed a sky blue as an Italian lake, with just one white cloud, foamy-edged as spray.

And all she could think was "The Dandover is coming. With its priceless pearls." And, "The end

is in sight, and all this hypocrisy almost finished."
It was like being tracked by the serpent of greed
—even into the beauty of Paradise.

She stared up at the beeches above her head.
A bird was singing there.

"Wouldn't it be nice if we had been birds, Billy?"
she asked him, honestly, sick of it all.

Billy laughed.

"It's all right to be humans," he said, wisely.
"Don't you think so? You ought to—young,
beautiful, beloved by me," and he laughed in
mock conceit. "Isn't it all right, being humans?"

He took her hand in his, sticking to it,
possessively.

"For some humans," she answered him, with
sad wisdom. "Yes. I suppose—for some."

"For you also," asserted Billy. "You know I have
asked you no questions as to how you came to
meet these crooks."

"No," she admitted. "You have been very
generous."

She attempted to get free her hand.

Billy relinquished it at once with the same
disappointed look, the puzzled wistful look, she
had come to dread. Here amidst the beauty of
Nature's pure world, leaf, and bud, and flower,
and tumbling stream, he had imagined he would
break through this troubled reserve which had
been like a stone wall between them. Did he not
know that she was in with a lot of crooks? Had he
not offered her new life, new hope, new everything,
in a world yet young? She had brought back his
Aunt's necklace in token of a new beginning, so he
thought—thinking the best, because he was Billy.

"Yes. You have been very generous," she said, almost grudgingly. "You can always remember that as a human being, at least, I thank you. But the *crooks* you speak of, Billy, you will never know how human they were, too, because—well, you have never known them. Perhaps you never will know them."

"Well, then, since I have been generous to you," said Billy, teasingly, "why be mean to me? Surely one kiss—"

She jumped up, suddenly.

"Let's take that path over there," she said, with forced enthusiasm. "It looks nicer than here."

Billy fell in with it.

But he had perceived the manoeuvre. She was sure of it. And it suddenly became terrible to her, hoodwinking him all the way, playing the penitent, when Shaney was planning the biggest scoop at the Reception which had ever shocked the unthinking world Billy lived in—a world which, stupidly blind or callously indifferent, took its "profits," but resented when the same reprisal was made upon it. The chaos, the panic, the hubbub there would be! The disgrace for Billy, and the blow—from which he would either recover, and marry Carminetta, or go down under, and lose faith in woman. She saw it all as she sauntered lightly under the branches of beechen green, his arm chivalrously lifted up so that she might walk under without bending her head. He stopped suddenly in the middle of a sunlit path.

"I wonder if you would love me if I were a beggar," he said.

It was a relief to find that he took the fact of her loving him now for granted. She blessed his cheerful conceit. Shaney was rather conceited, but he had never made that mistake, and it was part of Shaney's character that he went after a thing the more it showed itself capable of resistance.

She did not answer at once, but laughed lightly.

"I cannot imagine a Billy Durant begging," she replied presently, a shadow in her eyes.

But he made her stop, and gripped her hand.

"I am a beggar now but for the fact of your love," he told her. "Quite worthless from a point of serving my fellows, Lydia, but I mean to alter that. As Browning sings it, I was only an empty sheath of a man before you came, now there's a sword in the sheath. Still, we'll leave that for the moment. But if I were a beggar, Lydia—rags, miseries, sordid to look at, do you think you would still care? That is the great test of all love: to love on, just because one does love, for no reason at all. Would you, Lydia?"

She wished, almost religiously, that she had not come.

"Oh, yes, sure of it," she told him. "If you'd the same eyes, Billykins."

She linked her arm in his.

He pressed it against his side, perfectly happy—and she wanted suddenly to scream. She envied Slimmy, who, after all, had only to get through pantry windows, and wait for the "spoof" being handed in to him, and out again like a bit of lightning. She envied Shaney, who had only to think the whole plan out in cold blood, and then put his puppets through their movements, pulling the strings. She envied Ginger, and the others, who had only to hand in their reports, at intervals. But this smiling into a person's face, and into a face like Billy's, and speaking so nearly the truth that she scarcely knew how near it was the truth, or if, indeed, it was not the truth entirely—this was rather ghastly.

Billy began to hum from "lolanthe," the top-notch signal of his perfect joy. Forever, until death came, she knew, he thought he would remember this perfect day. Occasionally he looked into her face, with a boyish, "Glorious, isn't it?" They saw a pair of lovers, pretending to read from the same book; lovers in poor, shabby clothes, but happy, and honest, in this world of green grass and flowering beauty where all the grind and scramble was left outside. She envied them with a dull misery. Meanwhile, she had to drag him out of Epping without allowing one kiss. Which needed fine diplomacy. It did. But she managed it.

They sat on an omnibus-top, scooting back to the contradictions of civilisation. And she realised that as her coming into Billy's life had made it happy, his picking up of the Golden Garter was perhaps going to be the crown of sorrows to a life that had been all sorrows and "Thou Shalt Not's."

"You're rather sombre, for a young, young person, Lydia," Billy told her, on the bus-top. "By the way, I've never asked your age, but you are certain enough for me to risk asking it. How many years have you?"

"Tens of thousands, sometimes, Billykins," she told him, lightly. "Really I'm twenty-one in June." Quite suddenly, she wanted to cry, to cry over her own youth, spilled and wasted. But Billy was looking at her with shining eyes. She heard a quick breath.

"I took you for about eighteen," he said, delightedly. "And I'm twenty-four, so we can be married in the month of roses on your birthday. Isn't it a great idea?"

He smiled into her eyes, and the ticket man came for the fares, and did not blame Billy for having his fingers so intertwined with hers that he could not, just at once, find his change. And suddenly, like a vial breaking, the horror of it burst on Lydia.

She was climbing out of the pit of bitter callousness into which Shaney had flung her, a year ago, when he found her hand in his pocket, and made her marry him to save disgracing two country maiden aunts, who, prim and cold, had ruined her childhood—. Yes. She was in love with Billy, who was fumbling to find the fares, and saying idiotically to the ticket-man:

"Awful thing, being in love, isn't it?"

And it was the oddest sort of loving— the sort that didn't matter whether she ever saw him again, the sort that would make one glad to recall one had met him, the sort that would be a memory of goodness for ever. The sort that just saved—one's faith in one's own kind.

"I can't do it, Shaney," she told Shaney, two hours later.

Shaney smiled.

"You'll have to. We're all depending on you," he said. "I suppose that white-livered idiot has made you believe you love him. However, you'll realise the difference in his sort of loving and mine when we're settled in a nice, tranquil country place."

Lydia smiled ... tauntingly ... bitterly.

Indignation got the better of discretion.

"You dare to try and give me the slip, Lydia, and I'll—"

She was used to Shaney's bursts of murderous rage.

"Oh, how I wish you would kill me, Shaney," she sobbed suddenly. "Oh, how I wish you would, if you'd do it quick."

Shaney regarded her with eyes of wide and frantic surprise. Hell! She was losing her fear of him, and how could he hold her, then? If you had a slave who did not fear death, and invited it, power was breaking, breaking, and soon one would have none at all.

He tried another tactic, one he had never used before. Nothing like new weapons!

"Come, Lydia," he said persuasively. "It's just the last toss-up. The reception's due in two nights, and you're an amazingly fine actress, as good as any off the boards. Think! All of us have finished after this! Clean going, seeing it's such a clean world! Straight as (lies, all of us, and a little snug home where we'll be as good as the best leisured people, sort of influential in some village or other by right of the power money gives."

An amazingly fine actress!

She leaped suddenly to her feet, bringing her face close to Shaney's.

"I'll be dead, Shaney, dead before I'll act the hypocrite with you to my life's end!" she shouted at him. "Yes. I will. Some day I'll stand on the house-roof, if I go with you, and trumpet what you *are* to the world, you whited sepulchre! You devil in human shape. Someday I'll tell the truth, just the plain truth, whatever you do to me."

The footman came running in to find Shaney with his hands on her throat.

He pulled Shaney off, hurling him against a chiffonier, and a Greek vase was smashed to a hundred pieces.

The gangster surveyed them reproachfully. .

"You will make love," he said, reproachfully. "Under the most dire circumstances. Shaney, when all our destinies are tumbling in the balance, you will make love! Now the poor footman must sweep up the pieces, and I'll remind you that this is a furnished house at twenty quid a week."

Shaney glared at him and left the room.

"And I'm off duty, Jenkins, at seven," shouted the footman. "Slimmy's getting busy."

The telephone bell rang violently.

Lydia jumped up.

She could yet feel Shaney's hands on her throat. She was gasping for breath, like one who has had gas, and tears of half-strangulation were running down her cheeks. This was Shaney's "love." She motioned to the "footman," on his hands and knees sweeping up the pieces. She realised that she could not yet speak.

"I'll answer it," said he.

He left the shovel with the broken vase, and strode to the telephone.

"Yes. Miss Carstairs is out," he called into the speaker. "Any message?"

An answer came back.

The "footman" turned his head and placed his hand over the receiver.

"It's that fool Mallont," he said. "He's asking you to go over this evening and take the beloved with you. I'll tell him you probably will."

Lydia tossed her hair from her eyes.

"Wait!" she said, with difficulty.

"Tell him I've just come in."

The "footman" did so.

Lydia dragged herself to the phone.

She made a fierce effort, and after a few swallowings her voice rang evenly over the line, speaking in tones familiar to Colonel Mallont.

"How perfectly sweet of you to ask myself and Billy, Colonel. I'll come round about seven and get Billy, if I can."

Mallont's laughter came back to her, hearty and sonorous, "Do bring Billy. Mrs. Mallont wishes to see him. She thinks him a charming boy. We've just seen your photographs in the *Sketch.*"

Lydia gasped.

This was Shaney's stunt.

"And we hope to dance at the wedding," said the Colonel. "Our most hearty congratulations. And my wife is jealous no more, not after having seen Billy's photograph. So come along."

"I'll try to get Billy," said Lydia, faintly.

"*Try.* You could lead him on a thread," chaffed the Colonel. "Good-bye."

She hung up the receiver.

Then she stared at the footman.

"Why, isn't it to-night Slimmy gets in there?" she asked, with painful effort.

The "footman" laughed.

"You'll be there in the drawing-room entertaining them whilst Slimmy takes the impressions," he said. "Wonderful! Keep them well-entertained, Lydia. It would be a pity if for a little thing like this we should miss the big scoop in two nights, that will set us all on our feet."

"It would!" agreed Lydia.

She went to the window and stared out, wretchedly.

Slimmy. She could see him, barking away, with the fogs rolling up, "dead and done for" as he put it, crudely, if she flinched back, now. And on the other hand, there was Billy to be dragged into it. Billy, large and generous, and kind and clean, trusting her, and asking no questions. Just then the bell rang.

Lydia went and opened the door. The fine dusky blue of the evening was rolling up, London's night blue that seemed to make a carpet under the feet, flung down from the arc-lights, and the lavender song of old London sung by a husky-voiced lusty cockney came in at the open door. "Come in, Jim," she told Slimmy, slowly.

He came and stood with her, behind the half-shut door of the furnished house they would soon have done with.

"Let's hearken," said Slimmy, "Maybe I'll not hear that next year nor any year. Let's hearken."

And once again the pacing lavender-singer struck it out in all its plaintive tunelessness, which haunts more than any tune in the gloaming of a London street:

"Won't you buy my sweet blooming lavender?
Twenty blue branches for a penny,
For your pocket handkerchieves?
You buy it once, you buy it twice,
It makes your clothes smell very nice!
Won't you buy my sweet—bloom—ing laven—der?
For your pocket handkerchieves?"

"Go and get some, Jim," Lydia said, laughing lightly. "Go and get a bit, just to remind us of things that smell sweet, even when they're dead!"

Slimmy stared into her face.

It came out of the dusk cameo-beautiful.

"Yes. There's things I like to remember, too," confessed Slimmy. "After all, life ain't all cheating, is it? Christopher! I'm broke."

He stared at her, a disgusted expression on his face.

Shaney always kept Slimmy "tight." He said it was the only way to make him obedient.

Lydia opened a chatelain bag suspended at her wrist, and took something out.

Slimmy darted out into the blue dusk.

"Rotten luck, old man, ain't it?" he asked the lavender-seller. "Singing in streets like these?"

"How much?" asked the lavender-seller.

There was rum in his breath, sordidness in his garments; and he was selling blue bunches of memory and romance, without any consciousness of the irony of it.

"Gimme an armful," said Slimmy.

So they counted 'em up under a gas-lamp, and Slimmy said magnanimously:

"Keep the change, pal."

The lavender-singer stared.

Then he smiled.

"That's put me on my feet," he said. "Unfortunately I'd been foolish and spent what should take me to market to-morrow. But *that* puts me on my feet!"

Lavenderless and enraptured, he faded from Slimmy's ken. A fellow feeling makes one wonderous kind. Slimmy stared after him; then he heard Lydia calling, and went inside.

She took the lavender, and placed it in a great jar, breaking off two sticks.

"One for you, one for me," she told Slimmy.

Slimmy placed his carefully in his notebook.

He watched her place hers in between the pages of a book.

"I'll bring you in tea myself, Slimmy. Why, your coat's wet."

The steam was rising from him as he sat by the fire.

"Nothing," said Slimmy.

When she had gone he took up the book. He read in the fly-leaf, "From Billy Durant to Lydia Carstairs," and the date. The book was called *The Forest Lovers.*

Things that smelt sweet after they are dead, he thought. Yes. There were those things. He knew it. He had laid away a foolish dream. He had seen himself as he was. Things that smelt sweet, yes, that would always smell sweet, even when you were coughing yourself to hell! And one of them would be his memories of her, his fellow victim in Shaney's great scheme. Dimly his dream rose up again before him.

Shaney should not have her. He could kill both himself and Shaney, and since they would be two unknown men, no one would claim and no one wanted dead or alive, save the police; *her* path would be clear. She would be out of the whole thing, with scent of lavender to remind her of old Slimmy, and lavender in front of her, too. Sweet memories, ever in the making, with this lucky one, and all blooming and fair, as it should be, for every girl. Yes, every girl—only some didn't find it so, worse luck. He sat over the fire, staring and eating chlorodynes. He did not look like a potential murderer and yet he was saying, under his breath, as Lydia entered with the tray, "Me and Shaney— Shaney and me—and I'll fix up for him in hell!"

Lydia set the tray down.

"Slimmy," she accused anxiously, "you're talking to yourself."

Slimmy looked at her.

"Often the only bloke I have to talk to," was his answer.

"Poor old Slimmy," she said.

She sat down by the hearth whilst he ate and drank.

"Feeling nervy, Slimmy," she asked.

He shook his head.

"Don't worry," she told him. "I'm at Mallont's tonight with Durant, and I'll keep them occupied."

Slimmy's cup shook in his hand.

"There you are!" he said disgustedly.

"And I always feel safer on my own."

Lydia explained.

"I see!" said Slimmy. "Well, do your best whilst I'm there, but I'd sooner be on my own. If I'm copped there's only me then, but, of course, Durant'll be your shining shield. They'd never connect you with me."

He said it hopefully, happily.

Lydia laid her hand suddenly on, Slimmy's rather grubby, nail-bitten one. She looked at him sadly.

"Oh, Slimmy," she breathed. "What a gentleman you'd have been if you'd had half a chance!"

Slimmy looked thoughtfully at her over his cup.

"I believe I should," he said, philosophically. "But seeing I couldn't, I did the best I could. The only thing I'm worried about is to help you out of the smash-up, if there is one!"

"I know that, Slimmy," she told him, softly.

Then she laughed bitterly. "Who'd believe that crooks have hearts?"

Slimmy looked at her wistfully.

"Fact is stranger than fiction," he said. "H'm, yes. Who'd think that an object like me would lay his life down to see you steer clean out of this back to where you belong, where Shaney couldn't reach you. Rummy, isn't it?"

A sudden terror entered her heart.

She looked fixedly at Slimmy.

"Slimmy!" she said, firmly. You won't hurt Shaney?"

Slimmy seemed to shake himself, as though he had fallen into a dream, the old, haunting dream.

"No," he promised her. "I won't hurt Shaney."

He lied to her for the first time, and felt the demoralisation, keenly—more keenly than many a more educated person would have done. Already she was fading from him, he only saw her dim and far off, a beautiful dream he could not approach, but which he could save, even as he could not save himself. And, after all, had any man been able to save himself? Was it not always easier to save others? Yes. It seemed to be one of the laws of life.

"Now, your instructions and plan of the house are here," said Lydia. "I've just time to get ready. Good luck, Slimmy. Don't cough if you can help it."

Slimmy grinned cheerfully.

"Ram-jam full of chlorodynes, I am," he said. "Well, too-ra-loo!"

She held out her hand.

Slimmy lifted it to his lips, very quietly, very gently and kissed it as reverently as any knight.

"We're all human, ain't we?" he asked. "Yes. I reckon we are. Have I got everything?"

He looked round.

Lydia handed him a small parcel, labelled, "With Care."

She opened the door for him and let him out. A light rain was falling.

"Wait," she said. You'll get wet. Here's a coat of Shaney's. He's lots. Pop it on."

Slimmy popped it on. Then the door closed.

"Well, has he gone?" inquired Shaney, coming into the room later.

Lydia nodded.

"Yes. And you treat him shamefully, Shaney," she said. "He's no overcoat, and a cough like he has! Enough to kill him, getting wet through."

Shaney pulled at a meerschaum.

"He'd never be missed," he told her.

"Well, I lent him one of your coats. After all he's your cat's-paw, that gets the chestnuts out of the fire. So I lent him your grey mackintosh!"

Shaney stared at her.

"Oh, the grey one," he said. "Well, see that he brings it back, that's all."

He went out into the hall.

The grey one!

The grey one was on Slimmy and Slimmy would be sure to go through the pockets, and *her* letter was inside asking for money and saying, dash her, that one of the children was spitting blood and Lydia, Lydia would know, if Slimmy told her, that she was not married, but free, free, free, free to depart, free to do anything, free as any liberated captive since he was married before.

He stood by the hat-rack, trying to think. Slimmy would not search the pockets till after he got home, or perhaps not till morning. He must go to-night to Slimmy's lodgings, and get back the grey overcoat before Slimmy had searched the pockets and found *her* letter. Or he must, if Slimmy had seen it, bribe Slimmy to say nothing to Lydia. One could always bribe a thief. So thought Shaney the ex-schoolmaster who was supposed to have lost his memory, and to screen whom his wife addressed as Mr. Shaney: who had been Mr. Shaney, and all things, before he took in the rural authorities who wanted a schoolmaster cheap.

Slimmy, meanwhile, was paddling along to the bus and from thence to walk along the beautiful lane of Palace Green, where the trees were green and friendly and beautiful. And he stood under them for a minute to watch a faint star, one of the first of a night of stars.

CHAPTER VIII

A policeman, passing down Palace Green, saw under the trees, which threw their green boughs from a mansion garden to further shadow the glooming lane, a little man of the shabby artisan class, dreamily drinking something out of a bottle, and staring at the last red streak of sunset.

"Something good, eh?" he asked, jovially.

Slimmy grinned.

"Have some?" he queried.

"On duty," he was told.

Slimmy smiled as the policeman's broad back went down into the purpling night, with its networks of the lights o' London. He also was on duty. He placed the bottle of chlorodyne, of which he had drunk a quarter, into Shaney's overcoat and heard the rustle of paper.

"I'll look at 'em afterwards," gurgled Slimmy to himself.

He walked on, up the lane. A pair of children, beautifully dressed, laughing, came down with their nurse. They were talking of "Peter Pan." Slimmy only knew of Peter Pan by the statue in Kensington Gardens. His chief reading was Police Court news. He admired the happy children and was glad they were so delirious over life.

"After all, there *are* happy people in the world," mused Slimmy, without bitterness. "Happen some day there'll be a lot more. I'll be dead then, however."

He made a sharp detour towards the mansion of the Mallonts. Then he saw a taxi speeding along, and knew it for *hers*. He was leaning against the wall of a garden mansion as it shot past and he caught the profile of her face. He was sauntering past as she stepped out of the taxi with Billy and they stared casually at each other, without recognition.

Then, he saw her place her hand on Billy's arm, turning her face towards him as she spoke. As for Billy he had no eyes, he was blind to all but her presence. They entered by the front door, and Slimmy was left to enter as he chose.

Mrs. Mallont swept into the lighted hall.

"So you are the young lady whose Garter the Colonel restored," she teased Lydia. "This way, my dears." She led them into a large drawing room, all cushions and great chairs, and rosy lights, and the maid drew the casement curtains upon Slimmy, who was still "resting" against the outside wall.

"We are just a little family party," said Mrs. Mallont. She introduced Lydia to her niece, her niece's husband, and her niece's husband's sister, and a cousin.

Lydia sat down in one of the delightful big chairs, a yellow cushion behind her head.

"Put your feet up, my dear," urged her hostess. "Don't you find London tires your feet, now the warm weather is coming? I do. Every time I go to the city, I say, 'Never again. You're getting old, my dear,' I say to myself."

She was a pretty middle-aged woman, with kindly eyes, who told Billy, "It was really you I wanted to see. You looked so handsome in the *Sketch*. I wondered if you really could be quite so. Aren't you proud of having landed him, my dear?"

"Quite puzzled, really," Lydia told her.

Billy's arm was along the back of the chair she sat in. She became acutely conscious of feeling like two persons, one of whom was nervous and ill at ease and wondering how Slimmy was going on, and the other who sat quiet, calm, and in a way, enjoying the colour, the light, the kindly ease with which these people surrounded themselves.

"There's a man called to see if we want anyone to call with vegetables. He's starting up," said the maid, at the door.

They heard Mrs. Mallont expostulating with her for bursting in. Evidently a new maid, new to the ways of the world. Mrs. Mallont went out, and they heard the little sermon in the hall.

"Tell him we don't want any. We have a tradesman," said Mrs. Mallont, severely.

The abashed maid went to the door to give the message. No one was there. She stared into the gloom. It was empty, sudden fear entered her mind. She looked inside the ash-bin, outside the kitchen and under the long towel behind the door. The man must have heard and gone away. But how London frightened her! One felt anything could happen in London. She retreated to her quarters, homesick tears in her eyes, dreaming dreams—long dreams, and forgetting the man who had appeared at the door.

"Slimmy's in," Lydia was telling heself. "He'll be half-way upstairs, now, to the Colonel's study and the escritoire."

Aloud, she was discussing music with the Colonel. It was one thing she always felt sure on. Music! Had it not been a haunting desire to sing at more than chapel tea-parties which had landed her, and stranded her desperate, with her pocket picked in the wilderness.

"Oh, yes, I sing a little," she admitted.

And away back, she saw the old choir rattling out the "Hallelujah Chorus" and amongst them herself as in some other life, singing, in plain straw hat, and a new blouse squeezed painfully from her aunts, singing, all else forgotten but the joy of music, "He shall feed His flock."

"Do sing for us, dear," Mrs. Mallont said.

Sing! She was all on edge listening for any sound that came from Slimmy, who might tumble over something in those dim upper rooms, and she was asked to sing!

Billy was already at the piano.

She thought and could remember nothing to sing.

"This," said Billy, appealingly. "I—you never told me you could sing," and in his eyes was all the joy of one who will hear for the first time the beloved voice singing, singing, singing; that greatest gift of all.

"Light the candles," said Mrs. Mallont's niece.

So Billy lit them.

"Yes. Sing this," he urged.

It was "The Jewel Song" from *Faust*. Irony of ironies, when she was tired of jewels, and all the agonies jewels meant!

On the first notes of Lydia's sure voice Mrs. Mallont was leaving the room to see to the supper. Mrs. Mallont listened in pure wonder.

There was silence as the song tumbled to its end.

"Oh, my dear, what a voice!" she said. "*What* a voice! But you should have it trained."

And she realised that all the training she had got into, an impoverished girl, following a dream, had been into Shaney's power, into a terrible trapped position.

Then she began to sing again, choosing the pieces which were most likely to drown any sound upstairs, if Slimmy did tumble against anything.

The terrible evening wore away.

"Oh, I am tired," she told Billy, as they went down Palace Green.

"We have had you singing all the evening," said Billy.

"Oh it wasn't that."

She scarcely knew how to get away from him quickly enough. Had Slimmy managed it? Was he safe? She had to stand, allowing Billy to hold her hand, before she stepped into the taxi he ordered to take her to the place which would soon be empty of them—birds of prey who robbed other birds of prey. And she was conscious of his eyes, loving and Billyish, and that he was saying, "Aunt expects you will be ready, Lydia, on Wednesday."

It was nearly over.

She felt almost breathless with relief.

Two nights, then the scoop!

"The Dandover is coming to outshine Aunt, in her *rubies,*" chuckled Billy.

She tried not to gasp.

The Dandover rubies were something unhoped for. They had expected only the pearls and the red-black rubies were coming. And Billy was so confident that all was given up and started anew.

"Oh I am tired!" she sighed. "Goodnight."

Suddenly, before she could prevent him, he touched her cheek with his lips, boyish and worshipful.

She put up her hand as though she had been struck.

"There! I half expect you to melt from my sight," he said, apologetically. "I feel —anyhow—I've that to remember."

She laughed, stepped in, called "Good-night" again, and saw the curb melt away, and Billy, and then altered the taxi-man's direction.

She gave Slimmy's address.

"Yes, James is in," she was told at Slimmy's lodgings, in the poor passage.

She went into the wretched jumble of *a room,* the fire choked with cinders and ashes, and Slimmy curved over it. He looked up.

"It's rubies, Jimmy," she said, after carefully closing the door, and seeing that no eye was at the key-hole.

"H'm!" said Jimmy, thoughtfully.

They discussed each detail.

Jimmy looked odd this evening, but denied that he had been taking too much chlorodyne. It had not altered the quick working of his brain. She had never found him so quick. He almost took the words out of her mouth.

"Yet all you'll get is a wretched three hundred quid, Jimmy," she told him, compassionately.

Jimmy laughed softly.

"Oh, I get much more than that," he said, in his husky voice. "But even that is life—life and hope, after only just being able to pay bus-fares and live in a hole like this. My lung'll heal out there, it'll buy me twenty years of life. And through all those years I'll be thinking, ' She's all right. She's free, too.'"

She regarded him sadly.

"You forget Shaney."

He almost snapped at her.

"No, I don't forget him either. He'll be happy, too."

He dropped the subject with a sudden distaste for it.

"Then I'll go. I'll see you before we say our good-byes, Jimmy," she told him, cheerfully. "The reception is at seven. I expect the others all know their parts?"

"Everyone," said Slimmy.

He took her to the door, and she looked back, to see him still standing staring after her, that queer look in his eyes.

***

Shaney was looking up sailings when she got back.

"It's rubies," Lydia informed him, dropping into a chair.

Shaney showed no emotion, though the Dandover rubies were beyond his wildest hopes. One had to learn to keep calm.

"There's a spot in Surrey will suit us," said Shaney, reflectively.

The others came in, turned from household staff to conspirers, and they talked until almost dawn.

"Did Slimmy seem ordinary?" asked Shaney.

Lydia eyed him.

"Quite," she told him.

Slimmy had seemed queer and excited, but she was not going to tell Shaney that.

"Well, I'll get a few hours sleep, then I'll see him for final arrangements," said Shaney.

Lydia nodded.

When they had all gone, she locked the door of the room, and lay down on the couch, and covered herself with the eiderdown rug, and made herself sleep.

Whilst Shaney was thinking, "Another hundred pounds at the most would shut Slimmy's mouth, even if he dared to tell her. And that's only a drop from the ocean."

Soon, soon, they would be away—away, where notes of that kind would never find him, where Lydia could not hold him at bay any longer by threats of disturbance, which might cause too much public notice. They would live the ordinary life of secure, and leisured people, respected for their possessions. He could see the bungalow, the garden, the chicken-pens, the beehives, the Sabbath calm of the place, the brooks— feel the great leisure enfolding him after great accomplishments. And, smiling, dreaming, Shaney fell asleep.

As for Slimmy, he read again and again the note from Shaney's real wife, poignant in its appeal, in its descriptions of her miseries. What a sword!

And he could swing it over Shaney's head at the moment of their triumph. After Shaney had paid them all their shares, of course. But he must *get it* back into one of Shaney's other overcoats, so that Shaney would never suspect he had read it.

Shaney was out when he called after midday.

And on the plea of seeking a match he slipped it back into a dark blue overcoat, without being seen.

"Only another day and a half," he chirped to Lydia, who was still busy with the jumper.

She acknowledged the fact.

"Then ta-ta all round," said Slimmy.

Her eyes asked him if he had forgotten that she would still be bound to Shaney, to follow wherever he went, since for her, there was no escaping Shaney.

Slimmy could have sung.

But all he said was, "Lydia, here's an address of an aunt of mine who you might think of in an emergency. One never knows. Life is queer. Shaney might be glad to go off without you."

Her eyes scoffed.

But she took the address, indifferently, much as a prisoner might accept a pin in the hope that it could batter down a ten- foot wall.

Slimmy skidded off.

There was much business to do.

Rubies are not changed into ready money by magic. And he had to meet Shaney at five o'clock.

Lydia, jumper in hand, answered the telephone bell.

It was Billy's voice.

Could she come? His Aunt was ill.

She got ready and was soon admitted by Billy himself into the house.

"She wishes to see you alone," said Billy. "She'll like you in time, Lydia—"

Lydia smiled ironically.

"Probably."

She went up into the sick-room, but almost got a shock. She had always seen Billy's Aunt well-preserved. Was this haggard woman, regarding her almost despairingly, Billy's Aunt?

"Close the door!" said the woman in the fantastic bed-jacket.

Lydia closed it.

"I suppose no appeal will have any effect?" enquired the drawn-faced woman.

Lydia eyed her, not without sympathy.

"I am to allow my friends to be robbed to save myself?" enquired Lady Durant. "Already several of them have been blackmailed in order that you withdraw blackmail from me. And Billy, do you mean to marry him?"

Lydia's lips remained closed.

"If you would only promise not to marry him," said Lady Durant, with wild hope.

Lydia surveyed her calmly.

"I promise you not to," she said gently.

Lydia saw the colour come back into her face.

"At least that is something," said Lady Durant. Then she said, "Poor boy!" thoughtfully.

She held out her hand to Lydia.

"I do not understand," she said. "But I'm grateful for that."

The maid tapped at the door.

"Miss Dawson," she announced.

Lydia prepared to depart.

"Oh, come in, dear," said Lady Durant.

Carminetta came in.

She had a fixed smile on her pretty face.

"I've just got away from Cheney. It's most difficult," she said. "But I told him you were ill."

Lady Durant surveyed her young friend, who had saved her from bankruptcy with Cheney's dollars.

Lydia was writing something on a paper.

She slipped it under Lady Durant's pillow, which she pretended to arrange. When Carminetta had gone Lady Durant took it. She read:

"Play fair. If you warn Dandover, or if you make us make a slip, you are in it, and you go down, too."

"Cat, indeed!" moaned the torn Lady Durant.

"But really, Billy, I must go," Lydia told him, firmly, by the drawing-room fire. "The next time I see you will be at the reception. Miss Dawson is looking for you, I think."

"Oh, Carminetta here?" asked Billy, in surprise.

"Yes. She looks rather ill," said Lydia.

"Well, I must go."

And she was off.

The horrible mess she had made of this household was borne in upon her. Carminetta and Cheney—it was ridiculous! But all would straighten out when she had departed from them. Carminetta was sold to Cheney who had freed her friend, or would be soon, much as a work of art is sold by an auctioneer. Somehow, the tangle would straighten itself out, when she had departed. Jewels! How sick she was of them! There seemed to be a curse on things that were dug out of the hell of earth by humanity and worn as symbols of greed, and power, and vanity. But for them, for her, who pursued such things, what they brought promised life, leisure and liberty.

If she could only escape from Shaney. But always there was Shaney. She went back and made herself sleep.

The great drama of the Dandover rubies would soon begin. Shaney came in and looked at her, sleeping.

Not much more than twenty-four hours and they were on their feet. He had seen Verdes who was to take the "jewels" to Boulogne and from thence where they were expected. Everything was in order. He sat down and surveyed her, realising that she could not escape him since there was no place for her to return to, and she had to share with him, or go penniless— which would leave her where he had found her, on the Embankment.

He yawned, and stretching himself in the depths of a great chair, slept himself.

They all went out to the Coliseum that evening. It was the last evening before the great scoop, and Lilian Harding was with them. She, also, had been very useful. Shaney complimented her, on the way to the show. She had procured the tickets of invitation. Everything was set and nothing had been overlooked.

They enjoyed themselves as people waiting for life or death often assume to do.

It passed the time.

They discussed their individual plans for the future.

Harding thought she should settle down in some boarding-house, by the sea, and read a lot in the winter. It was surprising how all their hopes were for quiet respectability, and that Harding, who had whirled through life like a spinning-top, should fancy she would like to walk by rough seas in the winter, content to run a boarding-house.

"After all, it's only been our trade. Now we are putting up the shutters," said Harding.

After the theatre, they had supper in a restaurant, just an ordinary crowd of middle-class people to judge by their appearances, and Shaney thanked everybody for their past work, much as a grocer thanks his assistants on retiring from business.

Then they went back to their several resting-places.

Soon the dawn would break over the city, its bridges, the shining river, its streets of hurrying workers, and it was for them, they thought, the last dawn of uncertainty, of great risks, of strain, and after that, they were in the haven of security, which so many had without any effort.

Slimmy seized Lydia's hand as they parted.

"If I don't see you again," he breathed, duskily. "All luck, pal."

Shaney grinned a little contemptuously. "I shall see you, of course," he said.

Slimmy was to be called on, to be paid last of them all.

Slimmy nodded with a queer look on his ace in the gleam of the street lamp.

"Yes. I shall see *you* again," he acknowledged.

They heard him barking his way, having to walk. Shaney was keeping Slimmy penniless to the end, considering it a necessity. But into Slimmy's hot, dry hand Lydia had slipped half-a-crown, and Slimmy, after he had got from their. sight, hailed a taxi, like the best, and sat back in it, laughing softly, laughing noiselessly.

"Yes. I shall see you again," he murmured to himself.

"Yes. I shall, Shaney."

CHAPTER IX

A high-class band was playing classical music, screened by plants and flowers from Delier's, who had only asked that that fact should be advertised in the social notes. As Lady Durant wrote these herself, it was easy, "Who is that superb young man sitting like Achilles surveying the enemy's tents?" enquired *the* Dandover, as Billy termed her.

"That? Oh, that is the Hon. Philip Wentworth," replied her friend. "Would you like to be introduced?"

"Immensely," answered the Dandover.

She swept towards Shaney like a peacock in full sail. And, really, she was not unlike that bird. Shot chiffon over gold tussore was spangled as with dew-drops. Upon her well-fleshed neck, massaged newly for the occasion (by a private masseuse at five guineas), lay the Dandover rubies, red-black, mysterious, with their strange history and the legend of a king and his favourite haunting each magnificent blob, which seemed at times like beasts' blood as the lights caught them, and then black, like a world's sorrows.

The introduction was duly made.

Lady Dandover sat down by the Hon. Philip.

She found him a brilliant young man whom she thought was destined to make a stir in the world. They watched the dancers together. It was like watching a rainbow broken up into revolving figures and by and by the belief that she could dance the new dances seized Lady Dandover.

"Come along," urged Shaney, persuasively.

He could see their "crowd" at intervals, Lydia, and Billy—Lydia flushed and radiant, Billy adoring, the rest with their "partners," and at times Lady Durant, whom he knew would be ghastly pale under the paint. So it looked, so it looked!

He was conscious that Lady Dandover was breathing a little hard.

"We will wait for the waltz," Shaney told her, tenderly.

She sat down, with gratitude in her look, Shaney took her fan with exquisite grace, and fanned her.

She felt once in subconscious anxiety at the clasp of her necklace. That relieved Shaney of the truly dreadful thought that she might have brought the paste duplicate.

He grew intellectual, and they discussed great writers. He bowed his judgment to Lady Dandover, who asserted that Miss Wilcox was as great as Shakespeare *in bits.*

Then the waltz struck up, to the air of the "Blue Danube."

"I wonder how many have danced to their destruction to this music," said Shaney, philosophically.

"Thousands, I expect," agreed Lady Dandover, complacently.

She had not waltzed for a few years.

Her partner was certainly an exquisite dancer. A perfect gentleman, if there ever was one, was Lady Dandover's verdict. She found Lydia and Billy revolving behind them, once. She was glad, in a way, that Carminetta had got over the Billy episode. She would be able to visit Cheney with her favourite next winter, in New York. To be a Durant was something, of course, but it was money that made the man to go! Shaney danced her until she was tired, gasping, and then led her to the conservatory and went for an iced drink for her. She wondered if he really could be any connection of the Wentworths of Chichester, and decided to ask him when he returned.

It was cool, wonderful, in the conservatory and they were playing the "Blue Danube" again. The dreamy echoes came faintly to the conservatory. And her wonderful dancing partner was a long time in returning. There would be a great rush, though, she remembered. She felt once again at the clasp of her necklace and then he was returning, and the next moment, she was lifting her hand to the iced drink.

Suddenly, a man in plain clothes rose from behind the palms and cried, "Don't drink that, madam," and then, how it happened she could not tell, there was a shot, a thud, and her partner had thrust her down, and torn at her neck, and she heard someone screaming—screaming—a long way off, and then laughed hysterically, realising that it was herself.

Outside the excited guests were searching the grounds.

The police had been telephoned for.

Lydia had turned faint and it was Lady Durant herself who suggested Billy should take Lydia to a taxi.

He did.

His eyes stared at her in the gloom of the taxi.

She wondered fretfully if the others had yet got away; if Verdes would be waiting for Shaney; or if Slimmy had got the necklace, and would see Verdes—and all the time she was conscious of Billy's eyes. He had not spoken yet. He seemed dazed, he was trying to believe it was not all a game, that something of it had been true. There were only a few minutes to undo all she had done to him.

"So, Billy, it is the parting of the ways," she told him.

His lips essayed speech, but no sound came.

She felt sorry for his dreams, going down in this mad moment just as hers had gone down when Shaney gripped her wrist and decided to marry her rather than give her up to the police.

"You mean—that all—it has been *all* acting?" he questioned.

His voice sounded old and his face looked suddenly haggard.

He shot out his hands towards her and she sat quite still, wishing he would strangle her.

"The bulk of the world is made up of acting," she said relentlessly. "Yes. I suppose so. At least one does the best one can. That is the law of your world and of my world—for oneself. Let us be honest enemies. Most enemies are much more honest than those who sell their friends under the guise of friendship."

She took out her cigarette-case, and lit a cigarette.

Suddenly the taxi pulled up.

"Yes. Durant. That's my name," said Billy, leaning out of the window.

"You have not seen a person who has been masquerading amongst your lot as Miss Harding?" enquired an official voice. Evidently they had been trailed.

"No. Only—my fiancée, who is here now," Billy told him.

"Right-ho!"

The door was slammed.

The taxi moved on.

They came to the whirl of Piccadilly.

"I must get out here," said Lydia.

Billy called to the driver to stop.

"You don't leave me here like this," said Billy, doggedly.

"Only getting some cigarettes," she told him. He got out with her. She went down a side street, and left him outside the shop. He studied the cigarettes, waiting in a deluge of misery, unconscious of the pouring rain, his overcoat over his arm. She was a long time. He went in after her.

"The young lady must have gone," said the shop-keeper.

Billy dashed out.

The moment he did so, the key turned in the lock.

He returned to the door and found he had been tricked.

There was nothing to do but wait. It was pouring, and several customers came to the door, and swore and went away. He walked round, and tried to see if there was some other exit, but only found that a row of old houses were built up against the back of the shop. Desolation, desperation settled upon him, the terrible fear that this was the end, that never again would he behold her living face. They could be escaping by a score of ways. A mad desire to ring up Scotland Yard, to give the trap up to them, with her inside, possessed him. But that was to hand over one's dream pitiful and broken as it was, to be dragged through the mire.

Suddenly he heard the horn of a taxi.

Dumbly moving out of the way, for he found he was standing on the traffic line, he saw them, packed inside it.

"Drive like blazes," he cried to the driver of his taxi.

He was obeyed.

But just as they were gaining a tyre punctured.

"They've slipped us, sir," said the driver, mournfully.

"Seems so," said Billy.

He went back.

Chaos reigned at the place which had been so lately a dazzling scene of fashion, youth, and pleasure.

"I am going to bed," said Billy to his Aunt.

"But, Billy, I must talk to you," she almost whispered.

"I am going to bed," said Billy. "The world may crash, if it will. I am going to bed."

"The rubies—"

Billy stopped her.

"Are no concern of mine," he said, sharply.

And went upstairs.

He sat by the window, smoking, without realising it, staring out of the window at this vast wilderness from which she was no doubt travelling, himself quite forgotten. He had simply been a pawn in the great game, and this was his exit, now. They had many places to shelter them. They might be two hundred miles away by dawn, for a car could do fifty an hour in the quiet of the night.

He went down at breakfast.

"The papers, Billy dear," his Aunt told him.

For a woman who had had a man killed in her house, she seemed anything but depressed.

He looked when her fingers pointed it out, the paragraph which told of the Reception; the robbery, and the shot detective.

And a little lower down.

The social note of a quarrel between the engaged parties and the broken engagement.

He hated it all vehemently with a violence that startled him. Hypocrites, *she* had called them. And she had been right, however unpalatable it had been. A sudden suspicion, more terrible than any that had shaken him, entered his head.

"You allowed these people here knowing Lady Dandover's jewels would go?" he questioned.

"Billy, dear," appealed Lady Durant.

Billy's gaze took her in, the whole of her, her hands shaking, as she tried to pour out coffee.

"I'm damned if I'll ever eat another crumb in your house," he said, quietly, "You bought your own security at another's expense. But after all, it's what we usually do. It's the law of our rotten idle lives."

She raced to him as he reached the hat rack.

"Billy, dear," she moaned.

But he tore himself away. The door slammed.

"He will come back in a little while, when his temper has cooled," she thought, wretchedly. "He will have to come back. He cannot support himself."

Billy was sitting in the Gardens, his head in his hand.

"Cheep! Cheep! Cheep!" said the sparrows.

He recalled her wish that they had been birds, not humans, because, at least, birds were honest. And he opened his wallet and found that he had just one pound. The cheque-book was behind in the bedroom. And that was what he had left behind him, with that life. He summed up his saleable qualities, with a pound between him and starvation. Frankly, not much. Then he went down into the city, and the glaring placards hit him in the eye.

"Detective murdered."

"Robbery at West End Mansion Party."

"Golden Garter Gang at Large."

So, at last, the decoy of the much advertised Garter was connected with this organisation of blackmail, robbery and now—murder. And in all this scandal and confusion, she was trying to escape, as he was, from the lives they had lived, from the necessities which had enforced corruption, and both with as much chance of success.

"Murder at West End Mansion!"

At last he got away from it.

The country was all about him, the rolling gold of the gorse on the commons, the only gold, so it seemed, that did not bring corruption and misery and degradation in its wake. He walked on and on, and on, like one fleeing from a pestilence, walking towards liberation, if not of body, of the mind and heart. And there were jewels of dew on the flowers of the commons, and he saw larks drinking them, and heard their evening songs. Whilst he wondered if she would escape and if somewhere, on some other day, when he had run to manhood, he might look into her face, without shame, no longer eating the bread of idleness, which she had often told him, in many ways, was the bread bought with the blood and tears of others. Mists crept over the commons, gossamer fire. The evening grew purple. The winds shivered the rushes in a pond, that cradled the first stars; and later the moon, looking down, had she been possessed of conscious sight, might have seen a young man, in a morning suit, sleeping, with his head pillowed on his arm.

***

"Come on," said Shaney.

He seemed to be possessed of the strength of a madman. He did not even realise that in crossing the last marsh she had lost one of her shoes. Already her foot was bleeding, cut by coarse grass. If she hesitated, he turned back, and dragged her along. It was like following a will-o'-the-wisp with a will like iron, a will-o'-the-wisp, who, as they had crossed the marshes, had been giving her his life's history. She knew he was mad, now, mad irrevocably. That he had been mad when he had gripped her hand that night, mad before he fled from the life in the sleepy village. And he himself had told her, now, of the stupid wife and the children who were always crying, and she saw them all, pathetic, tragic figures, as she followed Shaney, to wherever he was leading her, if indeed, he knew himself. There were moments when he was so preoccupied, she almost fancied she could have got away, but a curious pity for Shaney had touched her. And then she would have been lost in the marshes, which Shaney, at least, seemed to know so well. The salt tides came over them, he had told her, exultantly, the salt tides from the sea, and she would be drowned if she did not stick to him. Sometimes a night bird flew near, making eerie echoes to its jarring cries. Shaney's figure was becoming black in the purple glimmering, and against the blood-red glow of the marsh-waters. Sometimes he sang, boyish songs which he had sung as a child in these waste places, dreaming dreams of becoming a great man. She realised that but for a kink in his brain he might have been great and splendid, but alas! he was only a grasper after power—to use for himself.

"Come on, come on! We are nearly there," yelled Shaney.

Sometimes he seemed to dance, a wild figure, over the bobs of earth, from which he unerringly strode.

She glanced around the wilderness of water ribbed with earth. No habitation was, as yet, in sight. The crimson sky shot crimson into the water, and one could smell the salt tang of the sea, just as Shaney had said he had smelled it, long ago, when he read the tales of "buccaneers," a companionless boy, brooding on how to escape from his lot.

She hurried her steps after him, for he grew increasingly impatient. A bat went past her, with a whirr of its leathern wings, and Shaney laughed at her cry. For an eternity they seemed to go on, then Shaney shouted for triumph.

Against the sky she saw the outlines of a black and desolate building, which appeared to have been a farm-house. Towards this she toiled, almost collapsing. Shaney waited for her at the threshold. He took her hand and she tried not to shudder at his touch.

"Wait, till I strike a match," said Shaney.

There were times when he almost seemed sane.

"This way," he said, and guided her in.

The roof was gone from the room they entered. They passed into another, which had a roof, and stairs, broken stairs, which led to a room also with a roof.

"We shall stay here," said Shaney, thickly. "No one will look for us here."

Then the match flickered out, and all was black darkness.

"But we shall want food," she told him.

"Ah! We can get food," said Shaney. "Or at least we cannot starve for a few days."

She realised that he was indeed incapable of thinking for himself.

"Food," he, said, through the darkness, as though his mind had caught at a thought. "Food!

That's what does it. Yes. That's what does it. If we could have lived without food we would have been like gods. All the world runs amok, seeking food. Horrible, isn't it? Don't you hear the lost spirits who have sold themselves for food, wailing in the darkness? Women and poets—and little children— all like ghosts seeking food, clawing after it, great long talons on their hands, clawing after it, anyhow, by any means, but still to have food!"

She sat in the darkness, shuddering.

A water-bird stirred some rushes. They sighed, like the spirits the mad Shaney had mentioned. She began to fear that she also would go crazy, if she had to remain here with him.

But perhaps the greatest proof he gave her of his madness was the fact that he no longer talked of "love" to her, no longer attempted to clutch at her, and seemed to have forgotten that in this desolation he could break her to his will. There was the danger that at some moment he might remember. She was cold with horror at the thought. Virtue was still sweet, and decoy that she had been, she yet possessed the great virtue of having possessed her body, whatever had been infringed on her mind. She was not Shaney's wife.

As Shaney's wife, she had not been Shaney's wife, and he had waited for the quiet hour of triumph, when all else would be secured, and she would follow. The irony of the situation shouted to her suddenly. Here was a man with his goal achieved, with enough "wealth" in the box he had carried across the marshes to buy all he needed to his life's end. And he was unable to enjoy it. He might as well throw it in the marshes for the tides to cover. The wild marsh-fowl could enjoy it as well as he. For this he had planned, and schemed, and all was a lost marsh. Sanity had broken down under the strain.

The man was shattered and without manhood, wealth was nothing. She pitied him, keeping quiet, much as a spider shams death, lest it be destroyed. She was very hungry. Yet hunger did not seem to matter. She folded her cloak about her and wished he would go to sleep that she might also sleep, or try to think, for she knew they could not hold out much longer, She wondered if poor Slimmy had got the night boat. And if Harding would run her boarding-house for respectable trippers! She thought of her aunts, at this hour taking the candles upstairs, and praying for her, as she had no doubt they would, though had they been a little more human, all this would not, could not have come upon her. She excused herself no more. The mad moment had been when she put her hand in Shaney's pocket, fancying that was a way out of her plight, after having her own picked in the lift. That had been choice. All that had followed had been destiny arising out of that choice. She saw it all plainly.

Then she heard that Shaney was asleep.

She tried to sleep herself, but her nerves were too taut. The night, the marshes, became full of echoes. Her hearing was strained to the uttermost.

Suddenly a strange sound from Shaney startled her.

She found the matches and struck one, with trembling hands.

He was trying to speak, but could not, and his face all down one side was twisted.

It was a stroke!

Shaney was helpless.

A great terror evaporated in which she still felt human compassion, almost shame to be glad that he could not harm her. But a new terror arose, she saw it. She was here with Shaney no longer as his victim, but as the moving figure in what to do with these ill-gotten gains. And she could not yield Shaney up. She could not get a doctor lest detection should follow. For over Shaney's head was the shadow of a rope.

A horrible Nothing enfolded them in its mocking arms. There was nothing could be done but to wait for the dawn, the dawn, and perhaps the tides would come up, and over them both before then. She sat beside Shaney, all through the night, holding his hand, talking to him. Her voice appeared to soothe him.

She realised it, with a trapped sense of the inevitable. She had thought she could kill him sometimes and it was left to her to escape without him or to stay with him, to whatever end was in store. And she was staying. Such are the ironies of life.

CHAPTER X

Shaney stirred and moaned sometimes during the long night. Lydia seemed to herself to hear only that sound, and sometimes far off, a dull and distant booming, which she fancied might be the beating of the sea. Was it coming nearer? Would she and this half-dead man, with whom she had no bond but one of human pity, be caught like rats in a trap, and drowned, whilst the world slept? Would Billy, dear Billy, whom she now realised she had always liked, read of their being drowned in these lonely marshes, and think, after a pang or two, "Well, she was utterly shameless and graceless," knowing nothing of the merciless forces which had driven her across Shaney's path, knowing nothing of the hard, dry sorrow she was suffering here, the silence-haunted terrors. There would be none to speak for her—none to say, "She fell into this man's power and yet evaded it, true to herself."

She hoped against hope, one minute to be free, and the next to be drowned with her captor, still unconquered.

She sat weeping in the darkness.

It was foolish to weep.

She had not wept, really, with girlish tears, since Shaney seized her destiny, with all its youth, aspirations, and dreams, and used her capacities as a cat's-paw in his great dream.

She was free now.

But the sea might be rolling up to drown her, and if she survived, there was prison. She was twenty-one! At twenty-one one dared to hope to be happy still in spite of all, yet there was prison.

Her story, simply true, would be disbelieved.

"W—water!" gasped Shaney.

Water! And all about them was only the salt tides of the marshes, and giving him those, she might drive him madder.

"There is none, Shaney," she told him, compassionately.

"W—water!" begged Shaney.

She had only heard him demand, command, before, and there was something terrible in the very fact that Shaney, with thousands of pounds of worthless money pillowing his head, was asking not for wine o' life, but only for a drink of water, and there was only that salt with sorrow and madness. Big, stupendous ambitions he had had, and walked through fire and flood to gain his ends, and over everybody, and here he was, hunted and trapped, asking only for a cup of water! And, if he recovered, the rope for his neck.

"W—water, do give me," began Shaney, and then his voice trailed away, lost in his dried mouth.

She had no affection for him.

But a world of human pity was softening her heart for all the strange sorrows of pain-born humanity, which dreamed its large dreams, and whose ambitions walked over everything, even over other people's lives, darkening them, tearing them, laughing at them, and then asked, plaintively, in a garden of ashes, for a cup of water and found none, no, not anywhere.

"I will try, Shaney," she told him.

It was dark, pitch-dark, but she got the idea that consciousness was coming to him, that he could hear what she was saying to him.

She forgot that he was a thief and a murderer. She only remembered that he was another human being, appealing to her, in his child-like need.

She groped her way to the doorway.

All was black, pitch-black.

She recalled that there were foot-holes on the marsh into which one could slip and choke, mud-stifled.

"W—water," urged Shaney. "For Christ's sake."

She groped her way through the doorway.

She touched the rough outside walls, and the air, salt and fresh, blew upon her, tears in her eyes for Shaney, who had ruined her young life.

"I'll get some," she called back to him.

"Quick!" called Shaney.

Then he was moaning again.

She realised that she must get some. But where in all this salt marsh, bitter and terrible, like Marah waters, was enough pure water to quench the thirst of a possibly dying man?

She put out her foot, and it squelched into mud, mud covered up with gross darkness, which seemed to mock and taunt her, crying, "Shaney will go mad. There is no water. This is your punishment for running away from your aunts, to follow a dream that you could sing."

She was up to the ankles in mud, now.

Dark! Dark! Everything was black, void, hopeless, and she laughed hysterically to think she was walking blindly into this desert of darkness trying to find a little water for Shaney, who had ruined everything for her. She was tied to him by the bonds of their suffering humanity.

Once she paused, fancying his voice, loud and commanding, came to her. Once she wondered if she was mad, to be wading out in these marsh-tides in the vain hope of finding something to wet Shaney's lips.

She thought of the trial scene before her, if she lived through all this, when punishment for a girlish folly would be meted out and all would applaud the verdict, even Billy, thinking she had got no more than she deserved, when, had they but known, this one night of terror, and agony, and utter hopelessness had paid for that silly girlish dream to be a big singer, and for the folly of picking someone else's pocket because hers had been picked.

A night-bird flew over her head, and startled her. Her girlish shriek awoke the echoes of the marshes. She became obsessed with the fear that if she found the water, she could not find her way back to Shaney. She had still one shoe on her foot. She was going to carry the water back to Shaney in her shoe.

She staggered on.

Once she fancied she heard a stream running, and stooped down, dipping her hand into the water, and tasted, but it was salt, like the lees of all lost and polluted dreams. Then, once again she fancied she heard it, and tried again. But all was salt and terrible, and the water left a hot, brackish taste on her lips. She wondered how far she had got away from the ruin where Shaney lay, another ruin dark and terrible and shattered by ambition from all he had meant to be.

Then distinctly she heard the bubbling of a spring. She groped to the sound of it and sank almost to her knees in one of the holes of the marsh. Then she found she had gone past it. The sound came from behind her. She turned back.

And at last she was near it.

She took off her shoe, and refilled it, after drinking herself, for her own mouth was parched. She turned and walked steadily into the darkness back towards Shaney. Once she fancied she heard the chime of bells over the waters, but put it down to imagination, unless indeed it was midnight, and bells for some reason or other could be echoing on the windy darkness, from some coast-line village.

"Shaney! Shaney! I'm coming!" she called.

Terrors of the night had begun to lose their power. Only she felt that she, outcast, was taking relief to another yet more outcast, meant to be splendid, but who had failed, failed, as all men failed, and must fail ultimately, fighting only for himself, rank individuality, caring for none else.

Once she thought as she got nearer to the place from which she imagined she had set out, he answered her, in a strange bellowing roar. But after going on, and on and on, she realised, fearlessly, that she was cut off from even helping Shaney, whom she had once hated, but now hated no more.

Yet once again, out of the darkness, echoed that bellowing roar which froze her blood.

"It is Shaney. He has gone mad, waiting," thought Lydia.

"Shaney!" she shrieked into the darkness. "Shaney! I am here."

In this utter void Shaney became at least another human being whom a human being, however outcast, could succour.

"Shaney!" the marsh echoed back, with her own hysterical note.

She wandered on, her head beginning to reel. Mechanically, she yet carried the shoe in her right hand; mechanically, she tried to keep it balanced so that all her labour would not be lost, so that Shaney, mad even, might drink, and be sane, might have some comfort in this night of horrors that enfolded them both, though the had been the victim.

Little sparks of fire felt to be going through her head, and dancing before her eyes, like will-o'-the-wisp. All the old, barbarous tales she had found in old books in her childhood darted in and out of her mind, like snakes terrifying more and more. She fancied that Monsters would arise from the marsh, goblins with weird lamps, mocking her, and blundered on. Once she fell upon her face into the marsh water, and scrambled up, groaning, to realise she had lost all the spring water out of her shoe. She longed for a star, however tiny, one little white speck of light for solace in this inhuman darkness, but none shone.

And yet again, through the silence sounded that terrific bellow, which died away suddenly. And then, she plunged into it, and realised it for what it was.

It dashed into her eyes.

She took a frantic step backwards.

It was the sea!

The sea!

And she went back, back, back from its rolling. Knowing not what she moved back into, wondering if it would not overtake her or surround her, as if the dawn would never come.

"Shaney! The sea!" she screamed, just as though Shaney could hear. Whilst the sea plunged up, roll and roar, following her on swift feet, and sometimes she stood in the spray of it, wearily thinking, "I will let it drown me." But life clung, yes, how life clung, how impossible it was to lay it down with its burdens and its broken dreams, and let the sea go over one.

She still went back.

Sometimes she thought she saw lights swimming before her eyes, but perhaps, she thought, those also were dreams. Once she walked through a soft ooze, and then over stones, and yet the sea came up and she dared not pause, since it never paused.

She was getting too weary to go much further. Her will was breaking, getting wandering. Faces swam through the mists gathering on her eyes, through which the strange lights yet danced. Billy's face, dear, and generous, and chivalrous, and all-believing, her aunts' faces, firm and reproachful and condemning, and Slimmy's—poor Slimmy's—thin, and hollow-cheeked, and his eyes full of timid adoration, but above all, Billy's, the face of the one she had most deluded, and whom she had loved so dearly, she had at last deluded yet again, saying, "Yes. I never cared. That was acting, too." Which was the only brave thing she had done, it seemed now.

She got a lot of weeds tangled around her bare feet, and was too weary to stoop to disentangle them, but dragged them with her, over sharp stones that cut her feet, at least they felt to be bleeding.

Suddenly weariness completely overcame her.

She sank down on the stones, hearing the bellowing of the sea, as it rushed up like a roaring animal sure of its prey. A strange composure, a forgiveness of every irony of life, was her last conscious thought.

"At least, it will be rest," she thought.

That was her last clear idea, that, and a fleeting memory of Billy, who was somewhere saying, through the roar of the surf, "Did I not offer you a new beginning?"

Then she was conscious of sinking down into a deep void, full of silence, rest, and utter carelessness of what lay beyond it.

***

She was sometimes conscious of a dim light penetrating her closed eyelids. But mostly it was dark, and she was wandering in an attempt to defeat the sea, a big sea and terrible, reaching out to catch her. And sometimes she walked where all was green and fair, almost like Epping in Spring, and Billy's voice sounded on her ears, and she endeavoured to open her eyes, but they were too heavy.

Gradually life and pain came back, and realisation of utter listlessness. She caught the sound of voices, kind voices, simple and unaffected, always expressing pity, human pity.

But when she opened her eyes, the room was empty—a strange room, which made her wonder how she came to be there. A simple room, with little homely pictures, crude and expressive; with sunlight on the whitewashed walls; and a few nets, waiting to be mended; and the sound of children's voices somewhere outside.

Then she heard footsteps approaching. A woman entered the room, white-aproned, ample-bosomed, with quiet, kind eyes, and the largeness of one who has lived by the sea, and seen ships go down to it, and men who came back no more.

Her eyes shone with triumph as she saw Lydia's eyes open.

"Oh, dearie," she said, and promptly began to cry. Then she called "Ben!" from the door, and a small blue-jerseyed boy came in.

"Go down and tell your father to come," she said.

He went out, closing the door quietly.

The woman took Lydia's hand.

"Dearie! You are better. Now tell us your name that we may let your friends know," asked the woman cheerfully.

Lydia shook her head from side to side.

"Well, if you don't want," said the woman.

Lydia moved restlessly.

She was misunderstood.

She was trying—trying so hard to think what her name was, but she couldn't. It made her desperately unhappy. People did have names, of course. And she could not remember hers.

She tried to move her lips.

They opened.

But no sound emerged.

Her strained eyes showed her agony.

Dimly, horribly, it was driven in on her that she was dumb. Words formed in her brain, shadows of words, rather, but they broke up. She was dumb.

"There, dearie, don't try," said the woman, swiftly.

Later her husband came in and with him the doctor.

"Nervous tension," he said. "Memory is there, but submerged, and the speech nerve has failed to operate."

After several days Lydia ceased to try to speak.

She began to sit up in bed.

Everything was so peaceful, she realised that, that it was in strong contrast to what had gone before, something—something terrible.

She would watch the ripples of sunlight playing on the walls, as if they shone on water outside, and were reflected. She could count the days by the dawns and sunsets, as children do. She was conscious of deep peace.

She sat up and helped to mend nets one day.

People came in—kindly, honest, simple people,

who looked at her, and brought fruits and books, with pictures. She looked at the pictures, finding she could not read. But she darned for the many children and made garments, and sat sometimes by the white wall of the cottage looking towards the sea, wide and blue, and mysterious, and now memories began to form. She spoke once.

"Milk!" she called, to the fisherman's wife, as she came with it to the door.

That good woman wept with delight.

But she could not remember her name, or where she came from, or who her friends were. She was building a new life round herself.

The children loved her.

She would sit with them, on the beach, looking out to sea, as though she expected some ship to come over the horizon. She watched all the new life with eager, curious gaze. She learned to talk through hearing the children. She was dimly pleased that she could sew, darn, and help in the house, and sometimes she was moody, like someone puzzled, and trying to answer questions in her own frustrated brain. She would go down with Martha to the beach, and help drag in the lobster boats.

Once she started to sing.

Martha heard her with wondering eyes.

"Oh, dearie, you are a great singer," she told her.

Then she ceased to sing, and could do it no more, though all the neighbours had been brought in to hear her. They were kind to her. She had a dim gratitude, crude as a child's, for all their wonderful kindness. She tried to understand when they told her she had been there months, nodding her head.

She said "thank you," because the children said it. She was not unhappy, but there was always something she could not understand, a sense of a dark, troublous something she wanted to understand, and the weeks drifted by.

And then the storm came.

The storm in which they forgot her. Martha, and all the fisher folk, running out in the midnight, leaving her by the hearth, with the sand blowing in at the open door. A deep, sullen roar.

She listened to it.

Then she walked out into the night, closing the door behind her, passing along with the rest. She had heard something roaring like that before.

She seemed to be walking on the edge of some great discovery.

CHAPTER XI

Fine sand was blowing in the streets as Lydia beat her way along, close to the house-walls. Muddled as her mind was, she was conscious of an excited joy as the bellow of the sea came to her ears. But she was pulled up short by Maggie, her good friend for so long, aghast that Lydia had come out so ill-prepared into this storm. She vaguely resented the fact that she was always treated as a child. She had a sense of wishing to be allowed out in all this blowing sand and the salt spray that was ever coming on the wind, blown from the beach, whence came that deafening surge. In some strange way she felt that it had something to do with her and she could have cried when Maggie went on arguing with her. Then Ben came up, in his oilskins, solemn-faced, as he stood in the light of Weeldon's cottage window.

"'Tis a storm—a ship on the rocks," he explained to Lydia, as he would have done to a child. "Go back, and keep the fire in."

"Do," coaxed Maggie.

They were shouting at her to make themselves heard. There was an eternal clatter of feet over the spray-spattered cobbles. Sometimes they had to stand close to the walls, and shut their eyes, as a storm of sand was blown along the streets.

Slowly, sadly, Lydia took her way back to the house. She left them, so that she would not get in the way. She took out a big, brown net, and began to mend it, still with a feeling of something struggling in her mind as if to free itself. An old woman came in and knelt down by a chair, praying, praying for those at the mercy of the tides, and Lydia watched her as a child watches, going callously on, mending the breaks in the brown net. The rain had begun, and was slashing against the window.

Suddenly the boom of a gun made the old woman start.

"The signal!" she moaned. "Oh, the terrible signal. And my Tom be gone to the rescue. Save my Tom, Oh, save my Tom."

Lydia went on mending the net.

Once the old woman came and watched her— the waif who had been washed up on Fisherman's Rock by the sea. The doctor said if she could cry her memory would return, with feeling.

"Cry, my lammie, cry," said the old woman. "There be men a-perishing! Oh, the cruel sea! The cruel sea! It took my man, it took my youngest, an' now my Tom has gone out in it. Cry, my lammie, cry, for if ye cannot cry now, ye have no tears in your eye-founts."

She was almost demented herself at the thought of losing her one son, the refuge of her old age. She sat in the chair and rocked herself to and fro, moaning to Lydia, who smiled and mended the net.

"Cry, my lammie, cry, there be men perishing!"

When the net was mended she sat with folded

hands, watching the driftwood fire burn and flicker. The blank behind her mind was becoming painful. She felt something there was to be done. She stirred restlessly in her chair, and the old woman saw her, and talked to her as though she was a child. She resented it more and more, got more than ever that restless, burning feeling that something was happening out there in the streets, something dreadful, from which she was barred, because she could not understand. A man flung the door open and came in, in spray-wet oilskins. The old woman rushed at him.

"Billy!" she almost wailed. "Have they gone out?"

She did not notice the sea-waif put her hands up to her head, as she heard that name "Billy!"

"They have gone out," said the man addressed as Billy, sadly.

The old eyes questioned him.

"Your Tom, we could not hold him back," he told her. "They were sending up searchlights. He had seen a man roped to the mast waving a flag. They would not take me as I was newly-wedded. They pushed me back, and the old man and the women held me. God! To have to stand back, like a child, because one is wedded!" He suddenly bowed his head in his hands and sobbed.

"My poor Tom!" wailed the woman.

"He be happier than I," sobbed the man. He collapsed into a chair, wiping his eyes with his great hand.

Then it was that Lydia, staring round the whitewashed walls, with their creels and fishing-nets, suddenly burst into hysterical laughter as memory came rushing back—burning, dreadful, swift pictures such as the dying are supposed to see. Shaney! Billy! Slimmy! Where were they all? And what was she doing here, in a little cottage where an old granny was crying, and a great man, with a face like a sea-dog's? Then the picture pieced up the flight from London, the fear in the train, Shaney's nerves, his strange conduct, his dash into the country of the wild marshes, dragging her with him, his seizure, when she was most afraid of him, and her journey into the night to find water for him.

"My lammie!" cried the old woman, forgetting her own grief.

Lydia stared at her with an almost crazy look.

"Where am I?" she demanded, in a shaken voice.

"You be—" began the old woman.

"Name of the place?" requested Lydia.

The hysterical laughter was no longer shaking her. She was calm with a sad calm, which knew rest was over, for ever and ever.

"Sleshton, Little Sleshton," said the man.

The wind boomed against the walls as he spoke. They felt them tremble.

"How long?" enquired Lydia.

She almost screamed when they told her.

Three months! Three months, like a dead thing, with Shaney, if he had been recovered from the marshes, and not drowned, *hanged*. Not that that counted. Rather, it would lift a load. Only she was sorry for Shaney, and she could have spoken for Slimmy, if he had been caught, and besides, she should have been in prison herself, for had they not always shared each other's luck and fate? Three months! And Billy under a cloud, perhaps, from which she could have cleared him! After all, what had Billy had to do with them, and their way of living, or he with theirs? Nothing.

She sat in the chair, trying to think coherently, agonised to know if the trial had taken place, what had happened, if Billy was in the scandal, since she had been affianced to him; if Shaney's bigamous attempt had been blazened to a greedy and curious world; above all, why she had not been identified as one of the gang in the Golden Garter Scheme.

"You know yourself, now," said the fisherman. "Yes. We see you do. Don't tell us now. There be a ship on the rocks, and the boats be out. I be going back to see what is happening."

"Billy, don't go!" wailed the old woman.

"Must!" he said. "But I'll send Ellen in. They are going up to the rock chapel, to pray."

"I'll go, I'll go, too!" said the old woman. "You go see, Billy, and bring us news. Oh, Lord, the terrible sea! Why did You make it?"

Lydia roused herself from her own agonies of realisation.

She helped to put on the old woman's bonnet, and tied the strings for her, and fastened her mantle.

Billy went out, and the wind, roaring like a savage panther, blew fine sand into the kitchen, powdering the floor and furniture, and the spray in the wind battered the panes.

Lydia took old Betty to the door. They had to cling together by the wall, so terrible was the gale.

Another group of women came with lanterns, dim figures through spray and sand, and sleet, sobbing, praying, beating their way through the gale, their lanterns casting flickering patches of light over the sand-strewn cobbles.

"I go with you," said old Betty.

A young, strong woman on each side of her took each an arm.

"She be come to her senses," said old Betty, pointing at Lydia. In the great sorrow which brooded over them, their destinies menaced by the gnawing agony that those who were all their world, their love, their bread, their past, present and future, they scarcely heard the miracle that would have rejoiced their hearts, yesterday, as they mended their creels and nets outside their little doors.

"So?" said one.

Lydia watched them, blotches of dark, set round with blown sand and spray. Unhappy mothers, wives, and sweethearts, the sea might take their all, wash up their living ones, dead and stark, with salt tears in their eyes, but they had their sweet and brave memories of yesterday, when they mended nets in the sun, and were cheerful, with their hearth-fires burning for those on the sea, and the table spread to please those they might please no more. Happy, unhappy women, who had known honest love, great struggles, clean hardships, but, above all, honest love through all life's other bleaknesses.

And she?

She gazed into the fire of driftwood, made perhaps from wreckage that had come ashore in some such storm as this, and shuddered.

What lay behind her?

Ruined ambition to sing and make a world to wonder, dreams gone down in the deep of life! Her aunts far away, dim figures with tear-scorched eyes, weeping more at the disgrace than for love of her! Memories of Shaney, thief, and accidentally—murderer, who had hounded her with his lustful passion, with a wife whom he had left to hunger, and a bleak world.

And yet.

She laughed softly.

Shaney had never had her, body or soul. Always she had thwarted him, only the world would never believe it. Billy, neither. He would think Shaney had been her passion, secretly, and she—she did not know if she had loved anyone, was not even sure, in this hour of storm, this wild, backward look into the windy deep of the past mad year, if she had even loved Billy, excepting as part of a life to which she could never belong, peaceful, and leisured, and full of the joy she had come to ruin in trying to clasp. Plainly her duty rose up before her. To beat her way even in this storm to the police-station, and say, "I am Lydia Carstairs, the crook."

But why?

The great question surged in her mind again. Why, oh, why had no one found out, in a small place like this? Photographs in the papers, too. Shaney probably found on the marsh. Why had she not been linked up with the great Fraud, which Shaney had messed up by throwing in a murder?

Slowly she dragged herself to a mirror that hung on the wall. Then she heard the boom of a gun far out, dull, agonised, and turned away from the glass without a glance.

A ship was going down!

Men were drowning out there, in a sea like froth and ink, with a sky full of foam and darkness.

What did she matter?

She opened the door, and stood in the doorway. The rock-chapel up on the rock threw its light to her. Her mind, alive and clear again, pictured the fisher-women in the rude rock-chapel, with the boom of the waves coming up to it. Praying, they were praying for the lives of their dear ones to be delivered from the trough of the sea.

Boom!

The gun was going again.

She wept, hot tears, like those of a hidden geyser which scorched her cheeks, and put her hand up to dash them from her eyes, with her old impatience at being a creature who wept, like all women. Then something of the knowledge of what had happened to her, beat into her revolted brain. Her flesh was rough, rough, as though something had bitten into it. She dashed into the house, tore down the mirror, and in a blaze of merciless lamplight saw herself as the waves had left her, and the rocks, before washing her up to haven.

"No!" she cried, impetuously. "No!" But there she was.

She conquered the impulse to dash the mirror to the flagstones.

Great patches of scarred skin on her cheeks, that had been fresh and blooming. And her hair was snow-white.

She would not have known herself, but for her eyes and her mouth, those were the same. Beauty mocking ugliness all around.

She sat down and tried to think.

Prison! She feared it no more.

As well be in prison all one's life, where beauty did not count, where the living warm heart did not count in that echoing tomb. Somehow she had dared to hope that Billy might see her again, perhaps in long years, after she had served her sentence, and be some kindly friend, who would come, now and again, scattering sunshine in his Billyish way, and bringing his children to see "poor Miss Carstairs." But even that was shattered. What man, even in the name of friendship, would dare to startle his children by taking them to see anything so repugnant to the beauty-loving eye of childhood?

She buried her head in her hands.

Then, rousing herself, she went out into the night, beating her way with savage strength down to the shore, with its torches which were ever being sent up by the steady hands of courageous, comely women. Comely women! She was a blot on the face of the earth.

"Oh, you should not have come," they shouted at her. Then they forgot her.

They were calling to each other, "The boats are coming in. Oh, may they get away before it goes down."

The moon had come out, murkily, through a riven cloud, and the dim shape of the wreck could be seen, driving towards the rocks.

Dimly, too, the little boats, like crabs, could be seen, tossed on the crests of the waves, and as they came up out of the gulf, into sight, cries of fearful joy from the women mingled with the sounds of wind and rain. Then, with a crash that rang even through the storm, the wreck went down, and a wail of anguish arose, for it was feared that the nearest boats would be sucked under with it. But, no, they bobbed along valiantly, oaring their inches nearer to the shore, Where a glare of torches flamed up with even a greater anguish of hope and fear. Lydia lost herself in the spectacle. Forgot for the time being her barnacle-scarred beauty, and the dreadful past.

She stood with clasped hands, hoping that these women's lives would not be shattered, these simple, honest, hard lives; possessing only scant bread, home, and shelter so long as men could combat with the treacherous sea. A dim peace, a hope for others, crept like a streak of light into her heart.

For herself all seemed lost.

Not one dream of all she had dreamed remained unshattered.

But she stood near to the great beating heart of struggling humanity, and realised that she also was one with it in its infinite hungers and sorrows . . . and dreams.

And at last, after an eternity, one by one the boats were dragged in from the roaring jaws of death by women standing knee-deep in the waves, women who grabbed shadowy men, and wept and gave thanks and kissed with hungry mouths that seldom kissed those the sea had sent back.

They did not notice her.

She stood amidst all that welter of heart-love and passionate delight, clinging with homely, hard hands to its Love and Bread—a waif the sea had washed up, which the night would enwrap as she stole away. Then they were carrying half-dead figures, saved from the wreck, figures already dear to them because they had dared so much to save them, towards the light of driftwood fires, and food, and renewed life.

She beat her way, a solitary figure, unnoticed amongst the shadows, fighting sometimes that she might not be driven into the sea.

Sleshton!

She knew now why the name had sounded familiar. Her Aunts had sometimes spoken of Sleshton and the crabmarkets held in the open air. She was not far from home, then—from home. Dark mockery! All through the night of storm she walked, wrestling as for her soul. There at home, where all had known her, there, in her own place, she would surrender herself.

At noon next day she found herself nearing the village. Yet none recognised her! She did not go on to her Aunts. They would come to see her later, she thought. She walked into the village police station, with its white roses round the door, sat on a chair where Police Constable Fisher was fixing a new nib in his pen and tried to say, "I am Lydia Carstairs. You will want me."

But it was difficult to say.

Her tongue seemed to have dried up like a dry sponge.

"I—" she began, and the sound ceased.

The Inspector stared.

"Are you ill?" he asked.

She shook her head.

Everything seemed to be swimming.

"I—I should like a drink of water," she said, cold shudders running suddenly down her spine. Yes. It was very dreadful to surrender.

She received a glass and drank.

"I—I am," said she, and faltered again.

"Yes. You are ill," he told her. "Come near the fire. You have lost your way."

She shook her head and stared fixedly at the glass of yet quivering water she had set down on the table.

"I am Lydia Carstairs," she said. "I was used as decoy in the Golden Garter Scheme.. I left this village to sing in London over a year ago. I had my pocket picked. I was stranded, and afraid, and I starved a little, and got nervous of the men, and I picked Shaney's pocket and so I came into Shaney's grip and, if the trial has not yet taken place I want to stand with the others. I realise it is quite impossible to escape the Law."

"Carstairs—Lydia Carstairs!" gasped the Inspector. "It—you can't be—why, she was—"

He regarded the woman with the scars on her drawn face, with the white hair, with the salt of the sea dried on her dress, torn by brambles, and with great boots on her feet.

Lydia heaved a sigh of weariness.

The room spun more and more.

She tried to argue with the stupid man and slid gently down from her chair to his feet.

***

Police Constable Fisher went ten miles on his bike, to the General Post Office, and rang up Scotland Yard.

What he got was scarcely worth the trouble.

They informed him, officially, curtly, that Miss Carstairs had been innocently friendly with the Garter Gang, but on the information of one of their clients, who had been engaged to her, and whose word was uncontested, the village girl had been merely a small unknowing pawn, acting under intimidation, and the part she had played really negligible, and that in the public interest it was not requisite to drag her into the affair.

With that they rang off.

Fisher found his wife attending to the woman who claimed to be Lydia, the village beauty, upstairs.

Personally, Fisher had his doubts.

But later, when he went up, and the food was bringing the colour back, and the scars seemed less dark than they had done on her blanched face, and the drawn look was fading, he realised that it must be Lydia, this disfigured young woman whose eyes were yet beautiful, and whose mouth was Lydia's own.

Sitting by the bed, he broke to her the news of her Aunts' deaths. She did not pretend an affection she had seldom felt to the old miserly females whose niggardliness had used her youth as a drudge, and denied her even little girlish pleasures. Still some regret showed itself in her speaking eyes.

"And, Lydia, they left you everything," Fisher informed her, snapping finger and thumb.

She was unmoved.

Indeed, was there not an irony in the fact that their dead hands had been more generous than their living ones?

Fisher interpreted this into an unbelief that there could be much.

"And Shaney?" inquired Lydia, irrelevantly. "And—the money—the money in the marshes. Did that turn up?"

"Shaney was washed up on the rocks," Fisher told her. "The swag—I suppose the sea got it."

Then he returned to the subject of her Aunts and their legacy.

"They left you ten thousand pounds," he told her.

Then he grew jocular, as she stared.

"With so much, even with your injuries," he told her, "you will be able to get a husband. Don't worry."

Ten thousand pounds!

As the door closed behind him, Lydia lay back on her pillow, and laughed bitterly.

She had been unable to have ten pounds out of so much when they were alive, to begin to have her voice trained, and now, with this disfigurement, after having been through hell, spent and broken, even of inspiration to sing, she had ten thousand pounds worth of gold thrown at her! To sit on, like a personified ugliness from which humanity would turn. It was like life, she thought, just like life which mocks forever the dreams of youth.

She buried her face in the bedclothes and wept as she had wept long ago when she was allowed to see a garden, party when all the people had gone, and the Chinese lanterns were dark. Then she realised—thinking—that after all it would save her from—Shanies! That made her almost happy. It was worth scars to be saved from—Shanies!

But the terrible thought that Fisher had rung up Scotland Yard, that Billy would be tracking her down to see her like this, tortured her.

And next day she was gone—flying from the terror of Billy seeing her, ever again, with his living eyes.

The heavy veil disguised the scars, as some days later, fashionably attired, she sat in the corner of a railway carriage, boxes and bags strapped and labelled, riding towards the sun—towards a new beginning.

Whilst even as she rode, apparently reading *The Delineator,* Billy was wildly pacing the village police-station. Fisher argued with him, pointed out that Miss Carstairs had had some accident which frankly—

He faltered.

Billy glared at him, handsome, clean, vital in splendid manhood.

"What the devil do I care?" asked that infuriated youth. "Do you think it was her face I was in love with? Wasn't it the pilgrim soul in her I loved? Won't the worms crawl about us all some day and we'll be a mass of ugliness to shrink from? What the devil did you let her out of your sight for? Damn! I'll search the whole world for her: now, even if it costs me all my aunt left me."

There was madness in his eyes as he dashed out to catch the next train back to London. At least, a commonsense constable looked on it as madness.

CHAPTER XII

All fashionable London was pouring towards Covent Garden. Signorina Mascari, the new prima donna, the greatest since Patti, was to sing. Sing! Those who had heard her were reminded of the words recalled by poor Trilby. "To sing like that is to pray." Stars and the night, night of London under which what mysteries are enacted. Cars and packed tube-trains with these satin- cloaked dames, aigrettes in their hair, vanity bags in ringed hands, all going to hear Mascari, Mascari who was never photographed. Mascari, who stood before her audience, hands clasped behind her, a black mask over her face, and sang like the angels, if angels sing with such humanity, such noble passion, such poignant quivering sorrow, such attainment of exquisite joy. Office boys fighting in corridors, the winner to be treated to the hearing of Mascari. People sighing in little tenements, "We can't go to hear Mascari." People wondering why she wore a mask, bets on it in West End Clubs, cold critics losing their heads, and writing reams of enraptured praise and then, great surprise, Mascari singing without money or price, to reach those who had wireless sets.

Billy was going to hear Mascari.

Beside him, in the taxi, sat Carminetta, whom Cheney Willard had relinquished, at the last moment, saying grimly, "After all, what's the good of buying a treasure box if there's nothing in the box? But if ever you find you *do* care—"

And he had given her his Long Island address.

"Have one, Carminetta? ' asked Billy. He offered her his cigarette case.

She shook her head.

She was beginning to realise Willard's common sense.

What was the good of a treasure-box, when the treasure was gone?

Yet he was all politeness, and unselfish thought and there had been nothing lacking *in their* engagement, to the visible eye.

Only even Willard could kiss more fervently than Billy could, at least.

But, then, when Billy had recovered from his long illness, perhaps—

So their taxi glided through the throng of taxis, all holding their humanity, everyone a whole drama in what it contained.

Into the packed place, thousands of pairs of eyes staring on the spot where Mascari would appear in the bluey-green dress she always wore, reminiscent of a sea, slim for a singer out of whom such notes poured, simple and without mannerisms, and forgetful of herself, like a voice, a disembodied soul singing, for the world's healing. Billy felt he needed healing this night. At last he had abandoned hope of ever finding Lydia. Like the broken shells of the shore, she had been swirled away into nothingness. There was Carminetta and quiet living, love, of a kind, the kind that is average, and kind, and not too romantic, but not the kind that had hunted for a soul feverishly over the seven seas, and around the earth, leaving him with just enough to begin life in suburbia, unminding dullness, since all was dullness now.

He settled himself in the seat, and opened his programme.

The orchestra came and played the music of Liszt.

He arranged Carminetta's cloak over her chair, was careful not to crumple it, bought chocolates, and wondered if Mascari's golden voice could bring any comfort to a Durant who could not relinquish a dream, a dream, for whom he had sought, even amongst the outcast women ready to pick it up, until Carminetta had pointed out that Lydia was too ugly to follow that trade, and anyhow she would have her ten thousand pounds. Carminetta was a little bit of a cat sometimes, but only when his dream was in question. She had been gentle, lately, more like the old Carminetta.

Slowly the curtain rose.

A hush fell on the house.

She came on light feet and stood before them, to a thunder of applause, before she had sung one note.

Billy sat staring, staring.

Then he touched Carminetta.

She turned a mildly interested face on him.

"Yes, dear?" she interrogated.

Then, as she saw his face, she whispered—

"Is it, are you ill again, dear?"

Billy laughed a throaty laugh.

"No. That is Lydia!"

Carminetta regarded him with patience.

Often lately she had seen him dart after some figure in the crowd and come back with a shattered look.

"Nonsense!" she said, practically.

"That is Lydia," said Billy.

He was almost gasping.

"I am going out."

' He half rose in his seat.

"But where, dear?" she asked.

"To wait," he told her.

"But, dear—"

"No. I will hear her."

He sat down again. It was just as well. People were beginning to get savage round about the young couple. Then she sang.

Others sang too.

It was a night of magic, magic even to Covent Garden.

Yes, To "sing like that was to pray."

Before the end Billy went out. Carminetta followed. He was standing out there, in the beating rain, overcoat on his arm, forgotten, waiting for her; not sure, now, since she had spoken her thanks in that exquisite Italian, not sure if he was not going mad, since he could take a world's wonder for poor Lydia, just because she could sing and wore a mask.

"Dear," Carminetta told him. "You are getting wet through."

He realised all she had suffered.

He felt reckless.

If *this* was not Lydia, he would marry Carminetta, and have done with it.

A car was waiting at one of the doors.

"Mascari's?" he asked, casually.

One had to be cunning.

Mystery surrounded her.

The man nodded, in return for a cigar.

Then he waited.

Later, he found that Mascari had gone in a taxi. But at last, with Carminetta sent home to be apologised to afterwards, he got to know the hotel. Yes. But Mascari saw no one. She was tired. Unless she had an appointment.

"Yes. I have," said Billy.

He said it quietly and casually.

"I will take your card up," said the man.

Billy let him get to the top of the carpeted stairs, then went up, after him, and as he tapped reverently at the door, pushed him away, turned the knob and walked in, upon Mascari. She still wore a mask, but it was flesh-coloured and fine, She regarded him with astonishment, as an apparition. Suddenly, swiftly, he leaped at her and ripped the mask from her face, almost brutally. She put her little hands, with a sob, to cover her face.

"No, Billy, no!" she whispered almost, the great courage breaking, trying to keep her last little dream, that he would remember her as she was.

"Yes, Lydia, yes—"

He was kissing the ugly scars where the barnacles of the mud tide and of the world had bitten, defacing, biting in, pitiful, tragic.

"Yes, Lydia."

The man outside heard their voices.

She snatched madly at her mask as he knocked, asking if Signorina needed his assistance.

"Not in the least," said Mascari, coldly, haughtily.

He withdrew in wonder.

And they, they had forgotten the world, until Billy, taking her face in both his hands, turned it mercilessly towards the light, letting it beat upon it. Then he said, in his old Billyish way, "Poof! The skin ought to have been ripped off and flesh planted on. I'm surprised at you."

She made a little moue at him.

"I know," she said, amazingly. "But, when I came to think, it was a good protection. You see, men don't love—"

She paused.

"Only fools like me," said Billy, ungrammatically.

**

It was even so. Lydia Durant sang years later, without mask, and the scars were faint as old sorrows, which have faded into mist, which the sun of the years is kissing away.

Shaney had defeated punishment, by death— drowned in the marshes. Slimmy, sometimes from Slimmy, who writes as a small boy to his aunt in London, came letters full of talk of frozen lakes, sun, and of a pal of his he calls Louise. As for Harding, once the passer on of jewels to Verdes in the hottest runs with the police, she keeps her boarding-house by the sea, and the favourite reading of that immensely respectable woman, who is called Smithson, is curiously enough *Huckleberry Finn.* So does humanity change with time, travelling towards its haven.

Carminetta accepted Willard, who taught her to forgive Billy. The Dandover has decided to include Billy in her will, since Mascari's singing fortune might otherwise make him feel small. So Lady Dandover, judging as the world judges. She tells Mascari, sometimes, she is rather like a person Billy was in love with in his salad days, and it is a matter of surprise to her that Mascari shows so little jealousy. For Carminetta kept her word.

None but Billy and she knew that the singer who took London by storm is the same who, under the knife of circumstances, helped to take it by storm before in different fashion.

The End.

www.ingramcontent.com/pod-product-compliance
Lightning Source LLC
Chambersburg PA
CBHW041752010726
47507CB00009B/369